LONG SHADOWS

COMMON LAW BOOK ONE

Kate Sherwood

RIPTIDE PUBLISHING

Riptide Publishing
PO Box 1537
Burnsville, NC 28714
www.riptidepublishing.com

Long Shadows

Cover art: Natasha Snow, natashasnowdesigns.com
Editor: Carole-ann Galloway
Layout: L.C. Chase, lcchase.com/design.htm

ISBN: 978-1-62649-526-5

First edition
January, 2017

Also available in ebook:
ISBN: 978-1-62649-525-8

LONG SHADOWS

COMMON LAW BOOK ONE

Kate Sherwood

RIPTIDE
PUBLISHING

TABLE OF
CONTENTS

CHAPTER 1

Everything was smaller than it used to be.

That was Jericho Crewe's first thought as he drove down Main Street. Things hadn't actually changed that much in the fifteen-odd years since he'd left Mosely, Montana: there were one or two new stores and a few missing, and an extra stoplight bringing the town's grand total to three, but otherwise, things seemed the same. Except smaller.

The town didn't shrink, asshole. His inner voice had never been kind to him, but he knew it was right in this case. He'd just gotten used to bigger things.

But now he was back. He pulled into the clinic parking lot on the edge of town and wondered again why the hell he was there. The woman who'd called him had said he should hurry, but that made no sense; if his father's injuries were serious enough to be life-threatening, he would have been airlifted to the bigger hospital in Missoula, not left in the clinic next to the fevers and gas pains and broken wrists. But the woman had sounded serious, so Jericho had come.

Now, though, standing in the parking lot, he was tempted to turn around, get back in his rented SUV, and get the hell out of Dodge.

Coward. Quitter. He wasn't sure if that was his own inner voice or one borrowed from his father, but either way it could shut the fuck up.

He made himself jog up the stairs of the redbrick building into the scruffy waiting area. There was no one behind the plexiglass at the reception desk, so he waited for a couple of breaths, looking for a bell to ring and finding none, and then took a few steps toward the back and leaned through the nearest doorway.

A young woman wearing floral scrubs lifted her gaze from her paperwork. "This area is for staff only," she said firmly.

He nodded. "Yup. Got it. But there's no one out here to help me. I'm looking for Eli Crewe. Can you point me in the right direction?"

She didn't seem impressed. "Who are you? Another cop?"

Jericho liked to think he didn't wear the job as obviously as some did, so maybe the woman was just making a lucky guess. Guessing that the police would have an interest in talking to Eli Crewe wasn't exactly a long shot. "I'm his son. Somebody called me and said it was serious. She said I needed to get here in a hurry."

The woman squinted at him. "Somebody called you? Who?"

"I didn't get her name. She said she was calling from here." This was getting annoying. "I'm sorry to bother you. I can get out of your hair if you can just let me know—is my father here? And, if so, where?"

She frowned and looked over his shoulder as if hoping the receptionist would magically appear and save her from all this. Obviously seeing no one, she exhaled deeply. "I don't know who called you. But there was no real reason for you to hurry. Your father *is* here, technically . . ."

He stared at her. *Technically.* "I'm going to need some more detail on that."

She stood up, threw another hopeful look over his shoulder, and then said, "Your father was brought here after his fall. But his injuries were too severe for us to do anything for him." She paused as if waiting for Jericho to catch up.

And apparently he did need that little bit of time. Not to understand what she was saying—he'd given enough family notifications over the years to recognize the patter. But understanding the words was different from identifying or controlling the emotions they caused in him.

"He's dead," he finally said, and was surprised by how level his voice was.

"I'm sorry. Yes. He was— The fall was from a significant height. Death was instantaneous. He didn't suffer."

Yeah, that was what they always told families, any time there was the faintest possibility that it was true. "I don't . . ."

"Would you like to sit down, Mr. Crewe? Can I get you a glass of water?"

Water was *not* what Jericho wanted to be drinking. His head was pounding, and he tried to find something concrete to focus on. "The police have been by? You made it sound like— Is there an investigation? What happened?"

The poor woman looked over his shoulder *again*.

"I don't know what happened," she said reluctantly. "The police— yes, they seem to be investigating. They've been here several times. They're arranging to have the body sent to Missoula for an autopsy."

An autopsy. So there was *something* suspicious about the death. Or maybe it was just the identity of the victim that had caught their interest. If there was ever anyone who could commit a crime from beyond the grave, it would be Eli Crewe.

"Was there an officer in charge of the investigation? Can you give me a name or anything?"

"Uh, sorry, I don't know. If you'd like to sit down I can try to find somebody who might know more. It's lunchtime, though, so I'm not sure who's around—I mean, obviously someone's with the patients! And there really should be someone at the front desk . . ."

"I could just drive over to the sheriff's station and ask." Jericho didn't want to go back out and sit in the waiting room, waiting for someone else to come and look at him with awkward sympathy he wasn't sure he deserved. He didn't want to sit still, with nothing to distract him from his thoughts and memories.

The woman smiled, clearly relieved at the thought of being rid of him. "Okay, sure, that makes sense. You know where it is?"

"The sheriff's station? Out on the highway?"

"That's the old one. It's empty, now. The new one's on the far side of town, last block before the trees start."

Jericho should probably be asking more questions, maybe about bills or making arrangements for after the autopsy or . . . something. But the woman seemed happy to let him go, and he wanted to get out of the building as soon as possible. He was starting to feel claustrophobic, as if the place actually *was* smaller than it should be and the walls were pressing in closer and closer.

So he headed outside, took a deep breath of cool spring mountain air while gripping the metal railing along the stairs, and tried to stabilize. He felt like he'd literally lost his bearings. Eli Crewe hadn't been part of Jericho's life for a long time, but he'd still been a presence, a lurking, unseen force. He'd been like the opposite of the North Pole for the needle of a compass; instead of being what Jericho had always been drawn toward, Eli had been the force Jericho had always been driven away from. And now he was gone, and Jericho wasn't sure what the hell that meant for his sense of direction.

You can still navigate the physical *world, you melodramatic bastard.* The sheriff's office was the only logical destination at this point, so he might as well make his way over there. Even in its new location, maybe it would be familiar enough to reorient him.

Two stoplights later, Jericho was on the other side of town and turning into the asphalt parking lot for the county sheriff's department. The town of Mosely didn't have its own police force, so the sheriff looked after the urban area, such as it was, in addition to a sizeable chunk of Montana wilderness. And it did all that with a pretty small staff. This building was bigger than the old one, but not huge: two stories, with bars on the windows to the left, indicating the county jail. The architecture was completely nondescript, just like the old version had been, but at least this one had the extra story.

Well, he wasn't there to appreciate the design. Still, he sat in the rental for a few moments, trying to gather his thoughts. His father, Eli Crewe: Tough, irritable, smart, and cruel. Sarcastic and sadistic. Dead.

It was going to take some getting used to.

In the meantime, Jericho unfolded his long limbs from the SUV and headed inside. He'd been right about feeling at home in the police station, even one that he'd never entered before. Just like his station in LA, the air here somehow managed to simultaneously smell sanitized and overfiltered *and* rich with a variety of scents: stale coffee, photocopier chemicals, and just the faintest whiff of gunpowder. He didn't love his job, but he'd apparently developed a soft spot for its trappings.

His shoulders relaxed as he approached the reception desk, up until he saw the heavy-gutted, gray-haired man sitting behind the counter.

Deputy Garron had been old when Jericho had been a teenager running around and getting in trouble. How was it possible for the man to still be on the job a decade and a half later? But there was no mistaking the jowly, pockmarked face or the perpetual scowl on it.

"Jericho Crewe," the deputy growled. He didn't sound surprised, just disappointed. "You're back."

"Not permanently. But, yeah. I'm here." He briefly considered trying to make peace with his old nemesis, but decided it would be a waste of energy he didn't have to spare. Better to stick to business. "I was hoping to talk to somebody about my father's death. The hospital said there's an investigation?"

The deputy was silent for so long Jericho started to think that maybe he was going to refuse to cooperate. But finally he shrugged beefy shoulders and rumbled, "Have a seat. I'll see if anyone can talk to you."

Not too promising, and Jericho wasn't ready to sit down quite yet. So he stepped away from the desk and wandered over toward the waiting area, which consisted of a long pleather bench, plastic ferns bracketing it on each end. The whole room looked like it could be hosed down if anything unpleasant happened in it. Good planning.

Jericho stood at one end of the bench, then slowly paced to the other end, then back again. He'd packed his running gear, thank god, so maybe when he was done here he'd find a motel where he could get changed and then burn off some energy. Running was always a good way to keep himself from thinking. Hell, running was a good way to deal with whatever happened in this damn town, and not just running for exercise.

"Jay Crewe," a female voice said, and Jericho turned in response to a nickname he hadn't heard since he'd left Mosely.

"Holy shit. Kayla." They'd been friends all through high school, and if their occasional groping and messing around had never quite elevated them to "dating," it had also never gotten in the way of their genuine affection for each other. Leaving Kayla Morgan had been the second hardest part about getting the hell out of Mosely. And now she was standing in front of him, wearing a uniform. He squinted at her insignia. "Jesus, Kay, you're the sheriff?"

"Pretty crazy, huh?" Her smile was as warm and open as it had always been. "When my dad retired last year, the community seemed to think it'd still like a Morgan in the position, even if the only one they could find happened to be female." Her face grew more serious as she stepped closer. "I'm really sorry about your dad, Jay. I mean, I know you guys weren't tight. All the same, though. It's got to be hard. I'm sorry."

"I hadn't talked to him for almost ten years," Jericho confessed. Cutting ties had been his father's choice, but Jericho hadn't fought the decision. At the time it had seemed like a great way to complete his escape, but now it felt like disloyalty, or abandonment. Whatever the verdict on that, he'd had no relationship whatsoever with his dad, and he didn't want to lay claim to an emotion he didn't deserve to be feeling, especially not with Kayla. "It's not like—you know. It's weird, but it's not a tragedy. Not for me."

Kayla nodded. "Okay, yeah, I can see that. So, come upstairs. I'll give you what we've got so far. And . . . look, Jay, this is kind of awkward, but the sheriff's department isn't working alone on this one. We've got significant federal interest, and they're likely going to want to ask you some questions. If this isn't a good time, you can probably put them off for a while, but not indefinitely. Might be good to get it over with."

"The feds? What branch? Why?"

For the first time, Kayla's expression wasn't easy to read. "A couple different agencies. Come upstairs and we'll get started."

Jericho followed Kayla through a security door and up a flight of stairs. She moved easily, clearly confident in her environment. Kayla had always been athletic and pretty, and neither of those qualities seemed to have changed with the added years and responsibility. She was still attractive by any objective standard. And she happened to be one of the few women he'd ever slept with. It had mostly been curiosity that had driven him to her back then. He'd known there was something not quite right, but he'd liked her and any pressure and friction had felt good to his teenage body, and Kayla had never complained. That was all it had been, beyond friendship, and it was long over with now. Still good to see her, though. Good to be reminded that things in Mosely hadn't been completely bad.

Kayla reached a doorway and stepped aside to let him precede her in. He felt a tug of apprehension as he realized he wasn't entering an office, but an interrogation room. That wasn't quite as friendly as things had seemed downstairs. He turned to look at her, an eyebrow raised, and she shrugged. "Might as well talk in here," she said calmly.

He frowned toward the mirrored window that dominated one wall and said, "And do we have an audience?"

"Would it be a problem if we did? And is it okay if I record our conversation?" She gestured to a beat-up old voice recorder on the table, but there'd be a video camera set up behind the glass as well if Kayla was as competent as he expected her to be.

He thought he'd left his issues with authority long behind, but he could feel his hackles rising. Damn it. Maybe it wasn't that he had a problem with authority in general; maybe he just didn't like small-town, small-time sheriffs who got high-handed for no good reason. He sank into the metal chair on the far side of the table. "I think I'm here to hear from *you*, aren't I? So, no, unless you're shy, I don't think I need to worry about an audience, or about a recording of what you say."

"I'd like to ask you a few questions as well. We're trying to figure things out, Mr. Crewe, and your cooperation would be appreciated."

Mr. Crewe. Downstairs it had been *Jay*. Jericho had no idea whether the shift was a message to him or an unconscious reflection of Kayla's new attitude. He didn't know if he'd been tricked downstairs or not.

He decided not to care. "What are you trying to figure out?"

"To start, maybe we could get some background on you? Where you've been, what you've been doing, that sort of thing."

"What are you investigating? I just found out my father's dead. I was told he fell, but based on all this fuss, I'm guessing the circumstances were suspicious. Are you looking at murder?"

"We're looking at *everything*, Mr. Crewe. Now, I think we have a fairly good record of your years in the Mosely area. Could you please tell me where you went when you left Mosely in June 1998?"

He frowned thoughtfully at her. They'd been friends. Good friends. Maybe he should be cooperating for old times' sake. But she'd made it clear that she wasn't asking him as a friend; she was asking as a sheriff. And he had a long and distinguished record of annoying the Mosely County Sheriff's Department. "*When I Left Mosely*," he said, as if it were the title of a story. "By Jericho Eli Crewe." He smiled, first at Kayla and then toward the one-way glass. "When I left Mosely, it was early morning on a beautiful June day. The air was cool, but scented with pine and something else—something I've always thought of as *opportunity*. I was a young man hungry for adventure, and I'll tell you, I managed to find plenty. But let's not get ahead of ourselves."

He leaned back in his chair and laced his fingers behind his head. "I hitchhiked. A common practice for me in those days, although it's been some time since I've indulged. I'm afraid the exact make of the car that picked me up is lost to the fog of memory, but I remember the ride being comfortable, the driver pleasant. He was a middle-aged man, overweight but not immense, with dark hair and dancing eyes."

"Mr. Crewe," Kayla interrupted. Her gaze was level, her voice calm. "We'll be typing this up and asking you to sign it, swearing that it's a true statement. Please ensure that you limit yourself only to those details that you can remember with absolute certainty. And please hit the highlights, rather than giving us the full picture."

"The problem is, Sheriff Morgan, that I have no idea what you're looking for. I'm trying to cooperate, but without any information about your investigation, it's impossible for me to filter out irrelevant details. So since I don't know what might be of interest, and since I *really* want to cooperate, I think I'm going to have to give you all of it."

Kayla stared at him, her expression unreadable. Jericho waited politely for a response, then after a few moments smiled again at her and at the window. "So, where was I? Hmmm . . . I'd better just start at the beginning to make sure I don't miss anything. So . . . That June morning smelled of pine needles and hope. I didn't have any breakfast. I've never been a big breakfast eater, really; I'm just not hungry for the first few hours after I wake up. Brunch, on the other hand, I *adore*. Especially a nice social brunch in a pub-style restaurant, one of those places you can go for brunch and stay all day, drinking beer and watching sports on TV and catching up with friends.

"But I left Mosely when I was too young to legally drink, so of course I wouldn't have been consuming alcohol back then. I do remember going to brunch at my Aunt Diane's, though, when I was a little kid. I don't think we called it brunch, but none of us were early risers, so by the time we all got up and ready to go and drove over to Diane's, you sure wouldn't call the meal breakfast, would you?

Or maybe you would. Is brunch dependent on the time of the meal, or is there a requirement of different foods being served as well? I'm not sure about that. I'm also not sure how to reconcile my love of brunch with my understanding of sound nutritional theory, which seems to suggest we should be *adding* meals to our daily routine, not taking them away."

Jericho was absolutely prepared to go on like that until his throat was sore, at which point he'd ask for some water and then start up all over again. But there was a sharp knock on the door just before a uniformed deputy pushed it open, strode into the room, and handed a sheet of paper to Kayla. "It's from—" He jerked his head toward the mirrored window.

Kayla took her time reading the sheet, then looked up at Jericho. "Eight years in the Marines, four tours of Afghanistan, several commendations including a Purple Heart and a Silver Star. You earned your bachelor's degree while serving. After your honorable discharge you joined the LAPD and are currently a detective in their robbery and homicide division." She frowned at him. "You couldn't have just *told* me that?"

"You couldn't just have told me what's going on with my father?"

A sigh. "There's a procedure for these things." She tapped the paper in front of her. "It seems like you should know how that goes."

"I know that the right procedure is the one that works. Did it seem like your hard-ass routine was going to work in this situation?"

She stared at him a moment longer. Then something in her gaze clicked off, or maybe on, and she sounded much more relaxed as she told him, "Your father was found by hikers at the bottom of a cliff in White Horse Canyon. We figured out where he'd fallen from, and discovered signs of a struggle. It seems like he was pushed. We're investigating all possibilities related to that."

Jericho made himself nod. Faced with the grim reality of it all, he wished he could go back to talking about brunch. "What were the signs of struggle? It's solid rock along most of that ridge, isn't it? Not the sort of terrain that would show footprints."

She paused, her gaze cutting to the mirrored window, then back to him. "We found blood at the top of the cliff. It's been identified as belonging to your father. And just spray, with no sign of what caused the injury, so our assumption is that whatever hit him must have been removed from the site, presumably by the perpetrator."

Yeah, that seemed like a reasonable interpretation of the evidence. "Is there a theory? Motive, suspects? Anything?"

Another sigh. "Plenty of suspects with plenty of possible motives. You can't be surprised by that. I mean, you said you hadn't spoken to him for almost ten years, so maybe you were hoping he'd changed after you left?" She smiled wryly. "He did, a little. He got worse."

No, Jericho really hadn't been hoping for a change. He'd just been done with it all and trying to escape from the frustration. "So, how has the investigation gone so far? All these suspects and motives—you been able to narrow it down?"

"The investigation is still in the preliminary stages."

"Well, where are you starting?"

Kayla's lips thinned. "We're starting where practically every Mosely investigation starts these days. We're looking at Wade Granger."

CHAPTER 2

Wade Granger. It had been a long time since Jericho had last heard the name, but apparently not long enough to lessen its impact. Luckily, he'd had a lot of practice at appearing calm even when his mind was racing. "Wade, huh? So I guess he hasn't changed all that much either?"

That was when the door banged open—no knock—and two men in dark suits strode in like they owned the place. Kayla visibly disengaged, leaning back in her chair and looking at the wall. He could sympathize: it was easier to not care than to try to fight the implacable power of the feds.

As annoyed as Jericho had been with Kayla only a few moments earlier, he suddenly felt like her ally against these rude new arrivals. He angled back in his own chair and squinted at the men. "Not cool enough for FBI. Not *quite* douchey enough to be Homeland Security. I'm gonna say DEA. Am I right? Do I get a prize?"

"Special Agent Hockley." The slightly taller, slightly older agent didn't offer his hand as he spoke. He glanced at his partner and added, "Special Agent Montgomery."

There was a moment's silence, and then Jericho leaned forward. "It's lovely to meet you both. I'm not sure I caught what agency you're being so special at . . ."

Hockley jerked his head in an approximation of a nod. "DEA."

"And *is* there a prize for my superior guessing skills?"

Hockley frowned and ran a hand roughly over his own face. "Mr. Crewe, forgive me for saying so, but you are not behaving in a way that we would expect from a man who has recently lost his father. Nor are you behaving in a way that appears consistent with your position in law enforcement. You don't seem to be taking any of this as seriously as we might have anticipated."

Jericho nodded. "That must be a little annoying for you."

Hockley's shrug made it clear that he considered himself too far above it all to be annoyed. "It's one more piece of the puzzle, I suppose."

"Must be a pretty big puzzle if I'm even a tiny part of it."

Hockley pulled a chair from against the wall and swung it in next to Kayla's. He sat down without ever breaking eye contact and said, "It *is* a big puzzle, Mr. Crewe. And we're just fitting in the last few pieces." His smile was greasy. "I thought I'd come in and make sure you haven't forgotten we're all on the same team, here. We're all law enforcement. But you're on the bench for this one. Sometimes I think we can get a little worked up, when our professional concerns overlap with our personal lives. So I wanted to remind you of your place in this situation."

"I surely do enjoy being reminded of my place."

Another oily, insincere smile. "It's not a pissing contest, Mr. Crewe," Hockley said with the complacency of someone who knew that if it *were* a contest, he, or at least his agency, would win. "I'm sorry for your loss. The sheriff said you've been out of contact with your father for ten years—is that accurate?"

It was hard to think of a smart-ass answer to such a direct question, so Jericho just nodded.

Hockley said, "As you've been out of touch with your father for so long, I don't think you'll have much to add to the investigation, but if we need any deep background, I will certainly contact you. Until then, though, please focus on your family. This isn't a time for you to be trying to solve crimes."

His family. Well there was Aunt Diane, she of the brunch visits, but Jericho had lost touch with her soon after his mother's death. There was nobody else, and Hockley probably knew it; Kayla certainly did, if she cared enough to remember. But it wasn't as if the agent was actually making a suggestion that amounted to anything more than *Fuck off*. "So that's it?" Jericho asked. Hockley might be done with him, but that didn't mean he was done with Hockley. "You're investigating his death as a murder, but that's all you've got?

Wade Granger is a suspect; is that just because he's a suspect for everything, or is there something specific tying him to this?"

"Mr. Crewe, your name has come up several times in association with Mr. Granger in the local arrest records. You were actually convicted of a few misdemeanors with him as codefendant. Is that correct?" Hockley didn't wait for an answer. "I've got to say, I'm a little surprised that the LAPD accepted you as a candidate after all that."

A Silver Star will go a long way toward making people forget dumb shit you did as a kid. But Jericho didn't feel like defending himself to this guy. "I guess they must have been pretty desperate."

"You hadn't been in contact with your father for a significant period of time. What about Mr. Granger? When was the last time you spoke to him?"

Jericho was once again glad of his training. He kept his voice level as he said, "Before I left Mosely." Right before. They'd woken up together, bundled into the same double sleeping bag that had sheltered them during so many nights out in the woods, and Wade had asked him to stay. Jericho had known he couldn't; if he didn't get away, he'd be lost. But he'd still been tempted, because being lost with Wade was surely better than being found anywhere else, with anyone, ever. "I left, he stayed, and I haven't seen or heard from him since."

"And do you plan to see him now?"

"Plan to?" *Hell, no.* And also *Hell, yes.* "I have no plans. Of any sort. I got here thinking my father had taken a fall and I was maybe going to have to figure out who'd take care of him while he got better. Something along those lines. Obviously those plans have changed, and I haven't had time to come up with a new set."

"Well, considering the situation, I think it's best if you stay away from Mr. Granger. And away from this case in general."

"Kinda hard to stay away from it without knowing what *it* is, but I'll see what I can do." He stood up. "Gentlemen, a pleasure to meet you. Kayla—" He let his face soften a little, but not too much. "Good to see you again."

She stood up. "I'll walk you out."

The two of them were silent all the way down to the front foyer. When they reached the door, Jericho turned and said, "It really was good to see you again, Kay. Seems like you're doing well. Congratulations."

She shrugged. "I've been divorced *twice*. I mean, once, sure. We all make mistakes. But twice? And I'm only thirty-four."

"Maybe that is a bit overenthusiastic. Any kids?"

"No, thank god. Not that I'm against kids in general. But being a single mom is hard with a regular job, let alone with a job like this one."

"Yeah, fair enough."

"And you? No kids, no . . . spouse?"

Kayla was a professional investigator; he knew she wasn't being nosy so much as she was gathering information, like a squirrel would gather nuts even if it wasn't currently hungry. But Jericho didn't need to feed tidbits about his life to Kayla. "I'm married to my work," he said calmly.

"As a police officer. That was a bit of a surprise when I first read it. But the more I think about it, the more I like it. The 'serve and protect' part of the job—you'd be good at that."

"I'm spending a lot of time on the 'investigate and write reports' side these days. But I'm okay at that too."

She gave him a long look, then stood on her tiptoes and stretched up to kiss his cheek. "I missed you, Jay. I'm sorry for the circumstances, but I'm glad you're back."

"I'm just here for a day or two." He didn't like the sound of being *back*.

"I'll take what I can get. Be good, Jay. And if you want to get a drink or something . . ." She pulled a business card out of her jacket pocket. "That's me. I can't always answer my phone, but send me a text or leave a message and I'll call you back."

Jericho took the card and carefully stashed it in his pocket, but he didn't think he'd be looking for it again. He'd left Mosely behind long ago, and it wasn't a good idea to start chasing memories, not after all this time.

So he smiled and headed out the door and down to the SUV. He drove for a while, aimlessly, wondering what his next step should be. A responsible person would go to the town's only funeral home to arrange some sort of service. He spent a moment picturing the crowd that would show up to Eli Crewe's memorial, if anyone showed at all, but he didn't really want to know. Instead, he steered the SUV out of town.

Mosely was snugged into a narrow valley between the mountains: a small outcrop of human habitation surrounded by almost endless wilderness. Within these confines the town was a rough grid pattern of streets, just houses and a few businesses, no real industry. There were only two roads out of Mosely—well, one road, he supposed, Main Street, that stretched in two directions. To the east, it ran toward the highway: civilization, law and order, the modern world. The other direction? Mountains, timeless forest, and freedom. He headed west, hit the wall of trees that marked the edge of town, and kept going.

He wasn't used to being in the mountains anymore, though they'd been his home when he'd been growing up. He and Wade had hunted and fished and camped out in all weather, both of them happy to be anywhere but in their respective homes. Now, though, the towering slopes seemed to be closing in on him.

And the feeling only intensified when he pulled off the gravel road onto the long driveway leading to his father's house. The trees were tight on both sides, their branches sorely in need of a pruning, creating the impression he was driving down a tunnel. The driveway was rutted and wet and the mud sucked at his wheels, trying to drag him off course into the branches.

When he reached the house, he was glad to see a little blue sky overhead, and tried to focus on it instead of the building.

There was only so much sky-gazing he could do, though, and eventually he made himself face the cabin. It looked almost the same as it had when he'd left: rough wood walls with paint so faded its color couldn't be determined, concrete steps leading to the front door. The gutter that had been falling down on the left had been repaired, but now it was sagging on the right. There was cardboard or plywood instead of glass in one of the upstairs windows, and a couple of stones from the top of the chimney had fallen away, leaving an exposed stretch of rusty stovepipe.

Stovepipe that was billowing wood smoke. *What the hell?*

Jericho eased out of the SUV. There were no other vehicles in sight, but there was no mistaking the smoke. Someone was home.

Maybe the bastard moved, and somebody else lives here now. But it wasn't likely. This cabin had been in the Crewe family for generations, and no one else would pay enough for it to allow Eli to buy anywhere else. Possibly the old guy had run out of money and *had* to sell, but somehow that didn't seem right. Eli was good at getting by on next to nothing, living off the land and bartering for what he needed. And for all his recklessness, he also had a deep strain of common sense. He wouldn't have risked the house, not if he could find any way around it.

It occurred to Jericho that he was thinking as if Eli were still alive, and he made himself walk up to the house before wallowing too much in that mental glitch.

He knocked cautiously on the door. "Hello?" he called out. The breeze sweeping down from the ice caps made him shiver; his blood had thinned in California.

There was no answer to his first knock, or his second. Well, hopefully it was still his father's house—he twisted the doorknob, eased the door open a few inches, and yelled again, "Hello?"

He saw movement first, and then as his eyes adjusted to the light, he realized there was a woman standing inside the door that led to the living room. She had dark hair, she was tall and muscular, and she was aiming a double-barreled shotgun right at his head.

"Get the fuck out!" she hissed. "I don't have it. Leave us alone!"

He froze. His service weapon was in the back of the SUV, still packed up from the flight. He'd felt stupid bringing it in the first place, as if he was going to need a Glock to help take care of his father. Now, he was wishing he'd been a bit more paranoid.

Or maybe it was just as well he didn't have the tools to play cowboy. This woman didn't seem like she'd be intimidated by a bluff. "I'm sorry, ma'am, I think I may be in the wrong place." He tried to speak calmly. "My name's Jericho Crewe, and I was looking for my father's house. Eli Crewe. He used to live here. I guess maybe he doesn't anymore?"

"He doesn't live *anywhere* anymore." Her voice was hard, but she'd lowered the barrel of the gun, at least a little. If she fired now, she'd catch Jericho in the chest instead of the head. Not a great improvement, but a step in the right direction.

"I heard about that in town. Ma'am, I'm sorry to have bothered you, but I swear I wasn't trying to break in. I was just looking for Eli's place."

"You found it," she finally said, lowering the gun until it pointed at the floor and stepping forward into the light.

He recognized a lot of things at once: the gun she was holding was his father's old Remington; he was pretty sure she'd been the one who'd called him in California and told him to get home in a hurry; and the ring that was glinting on her left-hand ring finger was his mother's wedding band. "You live with him?" he asked, not worrying about the verb tense. "You're—"

"I'm his wife." She stopped. "His widow. Whatever."

Jericho's brain refused to accept the information. He had no idea why he was so shocked. He'd just . . . For all of his father's negative characteristics, his one redeeming feature had always been his loyalty to Jericho's mother. She'd died when Jericho was in third grade, and after that Eli had shut down that part of his life. It was strange to think of him with someone else—loving someone else—giving Jericho's mother's *ring* to someone else. And this woman, tall and proud and fierce when Jericho's mother had been small and delicate and shy—*this* had been Eli's choice of a second wife?

"His widow," he said, and realized he'd have to do better. "I'm sorry for your loss. You're the one who called me, right?"

"Yeah. I thought—I thought you should be here."

Jericho wanted to ask why the hell she'd told him to hurry, why she hadn't told him his father had been dead on arrival, but he didn't bother. Grief and shock made people do strange things; there wasn't much point in dwelling on one peculiar action.

"Okay," he said instead. "Well, I'm sorry. Do you need any help? I mean, with arrangements, or with planning or whatever. Is there anything I can do?"

She shrugged. "You want to meet your brother and sister?"

Jericho froze. "My *what*?"

She smirked, amused and maybe a little sadistic. "Yeah, I thought that might catch you." She stepped aside, gun still casually cradled against her forearm. "Come in. They're just out in the woods. I'll call them."

Jericho stood still for a breath, then followed her down the narrow, once-familiar hall that led to the back of the house. A moment later he stood in the kitchen with the same faded floral wallpaper he remembered from his youth. The woman leaned out the back door and yelled, "All clear! Come on in!"

He didn't really expect any children to appear. It was easier to believe that this woman was mentally ill, hallucinating a family and maybe even a relationship where none existed, than to believe that Eli had fathered two more kids. That his father had given Jericho half-siblings and not bothered to tell him they existed. But then he saw movement over the woman's shoulder, two small shapes sprinting in from the tree line, and she held the door open as the kids darted inside.

They stood there staring at him, and he stared right back. He didn't think there was a family resemblance, but he'd never been too good at noticing that kind of thing. He did notice the protective hand the woman laid on each of their shoulders and the way they leaned into her for reassurance. He could remember the same kind of physical communication with his own mother in this very same kitchen, and for a moment he felt almost dizzy, as if he were caught in some weird time shift.

"Who's he?" the boy asked. He appeared to be the younger of the two, maybe five or six, with white-blond hair curling out over his collar. The older one, the girl, had the same hair but hers was longer and even curlier, tangled and clumped like it hadn't been brushed in living memory. There was a patch of brown near her ear that might have been leaves, or might have been something worse.

"This is your half brother," the woman said, as if the news wasn't world-shaking. "Jericho. He lives out in Los Angeles."

The boy squinted at him. "A brother? He's old."

The girl didn't seem too impressed, either. "What's he doing here?"

Jericho supposed he should step into this conversation at some point, but he was in no hurry, and no one else appeared too eager to hear from him either.

"He's here to help," the woman said. She finally turned to Jericho. "You want coffee? That's about all I've got to offer. Eli was driving our truck when he left, and the fucking cops have impounded it. They say there might be evidence in it, but I think they're just being assholes. Anyway, it's hard to get to town without it, so I'm not set up for entertaining."

"No, I'm fine. No coffee. I don't need anything."

"I suppose you should sit down, then." She gestured to the metal and plastic chairs around the old kitchen table.

He ran his fingers along the cool, shiny bar on the closest chair's back. "These are the same," he said. "A lot of stuff's the same."

"Well, some stuff's different too. I hope you weren't thinking you were going to come back and inherit everything. I don't know if Eli had a will, but I'll tell you right now, my kids need whatever money he had. They need this house. You'd better not think you're taking any of that away from them."

"No," he said quickly. "I wasn't thinking about that. Not at all."

She gave him a long look and eventually seemed satisfied. "Sit down, then." She pulled out her own chair, sank into it, and peered up at him expectantly, so he sat, bringing his face to about the same level as the kids'. They were both staring at him like they thought he might turn into a snake.

"It's nice to meet you all," he said. It was true enough, as long as he didn't go any further. "I don't think I got your names."

"I'm Nikki. This is Elijah, and this is Nicolette."

Jericho kept his face still. It wasn't like he was in any position to comment on naming practices, never having had the responsibility himself. "Hi," he said to the kids.

They didn't respond with anything beyond sullen stares, and he was hit with a flash of recognition. Not of the children themselves, but of their attitudes: that distrust of strangers, the desire to protect their home territory—he'd felt like that himself as a child. And these two were being raised in the same house, with the same poverty, at least partly by the same person. Yeah, he recognized their reactions. It would take more than a few words to earn their trust, and he wasn't going to be around long enough to make the effort worthwhile. So he turned his attention back to their mother.

"The way you greeted me at the door. That didn't seem— You seemed a bit hostile. Have you been having some trouble?"

"Some trouble?"

"The kind of thing that would make you answer the door with a gun in your hand?"

"I *didn't* answer the door. I had a gun because you were coming in, even though I *didn't answer the door*."

She had a point, there, but not a complete line. "So you didn't send the kids to hide in the forest? And when you told me to go away because you didn't have whatever you thought I was looking for—that was what you say to people when they come in without an invitation?"

She frowned at him. He waited. Both of the kids were watching, their gazes intent, clearly trying to figure out what was going on between their mother and this stranger she'd called their brother.

"There's been a bit of trouble," she finally said. "Before Eli died. And then again yesterday. Some men came by, searching for something. I said I didn't have it, but they didn't believe me. They broke a few things, said they'd be back and I'd better be ready to give it to them."

"And what's 'it'? What are they looking for?"

"I don't know. They just talked like I should, but I don't!" She sounded sincere. "I thought maybe—you know. Eli's businesses weren't always completely legit." She glared as if daring him to call her out on the understatement, then continued. "I thought maybe he had some—some merchandise, or something. But I searched the house, the sheds, everywhere I could think of, and I didn't find anything that looked like anything. I don't know what they're after."

"Did you call the police?" Jericho knew the answer already, but he had to at least ask.

"No. Fuck them. They wouldn't help. Or if they did, it'd be because they wanted an excuse to get inside and turn the place upside down themselves."

"Do you know who these guys are? The ones who visited you?"

"They're just hired muscle, I think."

"And do you know who hired them?"

She raised an eyebrow. "I have a few guesses."

"Any you'd like to share?"

"Well, I'll tell you who's at the top of the list," she said, her eyes narrowing, and he knew who she was going to accuse even before her lips formed the first letter. He sat there in his old kitchen, with the same metal chairs and the same faded wallpaper, and listened to her spit out the name as if it was just one more thing that hadn't changed. "If I was going to make a list, the person at the top would be Wade Granger."

CHAPTER 3

The bar had belonged to Wade's uncle, back when Wade and Jericho had spent time at it. They'd both been well underage, but there was a side room that functioned as a sort of club rather than a public space, and as long as they'd stayed out there, Uncle Mick hadn't minded taking their money in exchange for his watered-down draft and even-more-watered-down whiskey. Now, according to what Nikki had said before Jericho left the house, Wade was running the place, although she hadn't been clear on whether he owned it or just managed it. According to her, it was about the only one of Wade's many business ventures that was approaching legitimacy.

"I'm sure he still cuts corners and sells liquor that fell off a truck and whatever else, but . . ." She'd shrugged, obviously not too worried about any of that. If she'd been a dedicated rule-follower she never would have gotten mixed up with Eli Crewe. "That's probably where you can find him at this time of day. Or at least they'll be able to tell you where he is. Or get a message to him. Something like that—" She'd broken off in order to yell at Nicolette to stop peeling the wallpaper away from behind the sink.

And Jericho had heard all he'd needed to. He had no idea why he was getting involved, other than that Nikki said she had no one else to turn to. Maybe because he was a decent human being. Or maybe he was just trying to prove a point, to himself or to his dead father or to the world as a whole, trying to demonstrate the proper way for a man to respond to someone in need. Or, more likely, because hearing Wade's name from Kayla's lips had started a low, warm fire in Jericho's belly. And Nikki's repetition of the name had fanned the flames, and now Jericho was having trouble thinking of anything other than the heat that was and would always be Wade Granger.

Which was definitely better than thinking about Eli Crewe. So Jericho gave in to his obsession, drove down to the north side of Mosely, and pulled into the bar's roughly paved parking lot, then sat there and stared at the painted wood sign that was propped up on the metal roof. The sign still said, *Kelly's*, just like it had all those years ago, although Jericho had never known anyone named Kelly to be associated with the place.

He sat behind the wheel and stared at the front door of the bar. Wade Granger. After so much time, Jericho was going to see Wade again. No guarantee that he was behind the door, but going inside was the first step toward finding him.

Or maybe Jericho had taken the first step the evening before, when he'd heard Nikki's instructions to come quickly and hadn't tried to weasel out of the trip. He hadn't asked any questions, just booked a flight. Maybe he'd been motivated by a long-lost sense of responsibility toward his father, or maybe even then he'd been thinking about Wade.

He pushed the SUV door open and stepped out onto the faded gray pavement. There was a ragged paper bag blowing in the wind, ballooning up and bouncing against the chain-link fence at the edge of the parking lot, then tumbling down before a gust caught it and threw it against the wire again. Was the bag trying to escape the rough treatment, or was it willingly coming back for more?

It's a paper bag, asshole. Stop thinking so much.

Jericho kept his body loose as he crossed the parking lot and headed for the heavy wooden front door. He'd pulled his Glock and shoulder holster out of the SUV before leaving the cabin, and it was a reassuring, familiar weight. Why bother with a security blanket when you could have a handgun?

The metal door handle was cool under his fingers. A deep breath before he tugged the door open, then stepped inside and immediately to the left so he wouldn't be silhouetted against the bright outdoor light while he waited for his eyes to adjust. He was wearing jeans and a navy flannel shirt, a light windbreaker on top covering his holstered gun, but as soon as he saw the bar's half-dozen inhabitants, he felt overdressed. The jeans were too new and didn't have any holes, and they weren't grimy enough, and his shirt? What was he, some sort of pretty boy with his fancy *buttons*?

He scanned the room. The same dark wood paneling on the walls, the same mix of tables and chairs from an apparently infinite variety of styles. And the same clientele as fifteen years ago, or at least the same type. Many of them were watching him, but no one seemed familiar, and he wasn't sure if he was relieved or let down that Wade wasn't there.

Nobody spoke as he made his way to the bar. He couldn't tell whether the silence was because of his presence or if they'd all been quiet before he came in. It was three in the afternoon on a Tuesday, not exactly party time, so these men were likely serious drinkers. Maybe they didn't like to have their activity interrupted with mindless chatter.

"I'm looking for Wade Granger," Jericho told the bartender, and the silence of the room deepened into something ominous.

After a pause and a once-over, the bartender asked, "He expecting you?"

Good question. "He might be." After all, even if Wade hadn't been involved in Eli's death, he'd have heard about it. And it wasn't too surprising for a son to come home after his father died. If Wade knew Jericho was in town, would he be anticipating a visit? "Or he might not be."

The bartender scowled, and Jericho noticed how wide the man was. Fat, sure, but solid underneath it. And if he worked for Wade, he likely wasn't a pacifist. Jericho needed to keep his smart-ass tendencies under control. Just because he had a gun didn't mean he was safe; most everyone in the place was probably carrying.

So Jericho smiled. "If he's not around, maybe you could tell me how to get in touch with him? Or I could leave a message here, if that would work."

"I'm not his secretary."

"No, I guess not." Was this the universe's way of telling Jericho to stay away from Wade? Well, if the universe wanted him to pay attention, it was going to have to be a bit less subtle. Jericho slid his ass onto one of the barstools, the denim of his jeans snagging on the duct tape holding the vinyl cover together. "So I'll just have a beer, then. Maybe I'll get lucky and he'll show up."

"You allowed to drink on duty?" The bartender smirked knowingly.

Jericho kept his face impassive. Was he telegraphing his profession or had the bartender heard about him before he even walked into the place? Either way, there was no reason to give the guy the satisfaction of a reaction. "What's on tap?"

The bartender stared at him. Jericho stared back. Then he caught motion out of the corner of his eye and let his gaze be drawn over the bartender's shoulder, to the hall that led to the private room at the side of the building.

There'd been a man standing in the shadows of the hallway. Now he'd stepped forward just a little, enough to be noticed but not clearly seen.

But Jericho didn't need a clear view to recognize Wade Granger. Jericho's body made the identification, his blood singing and surging toward his once-familiar partner. So Jericho waited, trying to control himself, and Wade eventually took another step forward into the light.

He looked older, but in a good way. His hair was still jet-black, but cut short and tidy instead of curling down his neck, and his perpetually tanned skin was showing just the beginnings of being weathered as it stretched over his high cheekbones. His gray eyes were as bottomless as they'd ever been. The boy had turned into a man but hadn't lost his beauty.

Jericho had heard people call Wade oily, but that wasn't the right word. Wade was iridescent, sure, but he was quicksilver, not oil. He'd always been beautiful and fluid and impossible to hold on to. Fascinating but deadly. He'd been the only thing that had kept Jericho sane through far too many nights of desperation and rebellion, and he'd been the only thing that had seriously tempted him to stay in Mosely years before.

But Jericho had left, and Wade had stayed behind. Now Wade was staring at him, assessing him, and Jericho had no idea what he was seeing. He forced himself to remain still, and finally Wade smiled.

"Jay Crewe," he said. He walked slowly toward Jericho but stayed behind the bar, sinuous grace apparent in the simplest movements.

Wade was wearing black jeans and a gray dress shirt, black work boots tying him in to the crowd at the mismatched tables even as something else, something indefinable, set him apart. "It's been a long time."

"It has." Maybe Jericho should have found something more profound to say, but nothing came to mind.

And Wade nodded, as if appreciating the simple truth. He pulled two glasses away from a cluster on the counter and filled one, then the other, with beer from the tap. After sliding one across to Jericho, he raised the other. "Welcome back."

Jericho knew the drill. He lifted his glass to his lips and together he and Wade drank, draining their glasses in several long gulps, then flipping the glasses over and resting them upside down on the bar. It was juvenile, of course, but he'd been seventeen years old when he left Mosely; there hadn't been much call for maturity. Wade's smile was familiar and affectionate, and Jericho wanted to relax. Even if this wasn't real, even if it was just an empty echo of a relationship that had long since imploded, it still felt good. It felt fucking perfect.

But he was at the bar for a reason. "I came by to talk to you about my father. His wife. Their kids."

Wade's frown was too obvious to be genuine. He'd always been an expert at hiding his emotions, so if something actually appeared on his face, at least in public, it was almost certainly just for show. Unless Jericho was presuming too much, making judgments based on who Wade had been fifteen years ago instead of whoever he was now.

But Wade's voice was so familiar, his intonations exactly as Jericho would have expected. "Family? You'd better come back to the office, then." Wade refilled their glasses and handed one over to Jericho, then inclined his head toward the hallway he'd been lurking in.

Jericho let himself be guided. As a police officer, he'd been trained to avoid situations like this; it was never a good idea to be alone with a suspect, especially in a hostile environment. But this wasn't just any suspect, it was Wade. Jericho would take the chance.

"Excuse the clutter," Wade said as he pushed open a door. Jericho stepped into an office straight out of the fifties, with a heavy wooden desk and two leather club chairs and one of those stained-glass lamps hanging from the ceiling. There *was* a lot of clutter, mostly paperwork and liquor boxes, but the chairs were free. Jericho stood in front of one and waited; Wade waved a hand in a vaguely invitational manner and sank into the other chair.

Jericho sat. "I'm more used to barstools in this place. I didn't even know this office was here."

"I guess we're not young punks anymore." Wade leaned back in his chair. "We should probably be sipping a fine Scotch."

"I'm in town because of my father," Jericho said, and that was certainly enough to end the small talk and bring the conversation back to reality.

Wade nodded slowly. "I'm sorry for your loss."

"Are you?" Sometimes blunt questions could be the most effective.

But Wade wasn't the sort to be caught off guard. "I know you had some trouble with him, but he and I got along pretty well after you left." He sipped his beer and watched Jericho's reaction as he added, "We did business together from time to time."

"Business," Jericho echoed. He wished he *did* have a glass of Scotch, or anything stronger than beer to wash the taste of that word out of his mouth. "By 'business,' I assume you mean 'crime'?"

Wade smiled as if Jericho were a talking dog. "You always did have a tendency toward seeing things in black and white. Not a fan of ambiguity, are you?"

"No, I guess I'm not. And I know my father never did an honest day's work in his life. So if you were working with him, I imagine you weren't being honest either."

"I don't think you and I need to have a conversation about which one of us is more *honest*, do you?" Wade's smile was still placid, but his eyes were sharp.

"What? When was I dishonest with you? I told you everything. Told you what I was planning—" Jericho caught himself. Was he really going to try to dig up all that ancient history? What could be gained? He needed to control himself, and then control this conversation. "Look, whatever you and my father were up to—that's between you and him. I'm not—" Not what? Not interested? That wasn't quite right. "I'm not denying what he was. I don't think I want revenge, or justice. Not if he got killed because of shit he'd gotten mixed up in. He knew the risks. I'm just trying to figure out what's going on with his wife and their kids. Nikki said some hired muscle came by looking for something. I'd like to make sure that's all sorted out before I head back home."

"Home." Wade finished his beer and put the empty glass on the corner of the desk. "Los Angeles is home?"

"That's where I live, yeah." Jericho squinted at the other man. "I'm wondering how you knew that."

"I know all sorts of things, Detective Crewe. It's part of being in *business*."

"What about harassing innocent women and children, threatening to rough them up in their own home? Is that part of the business you're in?"

"You really think Eli would marry an *innocent* woman, Jay?" Wade's smile was lazy and insufferable. He waited for an answer, and when he didn't get one, he sank back into his chair, as if satisfied that his work for the day was done.

Jericho was left to think. *What kind of woman* would *Eli marry? Or maybe it's better to ask what kind would marry* Eli? And have two children with him. Nikki hadn't seemed too distraught about Eli's death, but maybe she was just putting a brave face on; she had the kids to look after, and other things to worry about. It was tempting to think that she must be stupid. Completely clueless about it all and, yeah, as he'd said, innocent. Life would be easier if Nikki was an innocent. But why would Eli have wanted to be married to that sort of a person?

Not just for the sex. Eli hadn't been a monk when Jericho had lived with him, and there'd been no sign that he'd had trouble finding female company to the extent that he'd wanted any. He'd just never seemed to want more than a quick fuck. Maybe he'd started having trouble finding women as he'd aged, and been driven into settling down? But Nikki was probably twenty years younger than Eli and it wasn't like he'd had a lot of money to hold her interest; if he'd been able to persuade *her* to marry him, surely he could have persuaded someone else to at least have sex with him without a ring.

The whole thing was confusing. *Everything* was confusing. Jericho had gotten on the plane that morning thinking he was going to be dealing with one type of problem, one series of emotional traps, and found something completely different, something he was still trying to keep himself from thinking about. Then he'd found out about

Nikki, and about the kids—his half *siblings*, for Chrissake—and now he was sitting in an overstuffed leather chair in the office at Kelly's, and Wade Granger was watching him with the same mix of affection and amusement and wry frustration that had so often been his response to Jericho.

"I don't know," Jericho said softly, and didn't think either he or Wade really knew what question he was responding to anymore.

Wade took pity on him. "I didn't harass Nikki, and I didn't send anyone out. This is the first I've heard about the whole thing." Wade looked at his empty beer glass, then stood and walked behind the desk. He pulled two tumblers out of one of the drawers, followed by a familiar bottle of amber liquid. No inquiry about whether Jericho wanted a bourbon; Wade just poured two and held one out as he walked back around the desk.

As he was handing the glass to Jericho, Wade said, "Did she say *why* the guys were out there? What they wanted?"

Jericho froze. The questions had been too casual. Jericho had been away for a long time, but he hadn't forgotten who he was dealing with here. Was Wade hunting for information, trying to see if there was anything going on he should take an interest in?

"She said she had no idea what they were looking for." Jericho needed to puzzle through that at some point and decide if he actually believed Nikki, but for the moment, he went with what she'd said. "When I opened the door, she had Eli's Remington pointed right at me."

Wade smiled. "Not the first time that particular piece has been aimed in your direction, as I recall."

"It was a hell of a lot closer this time." But Nikki had been a woman protecting her home, not a man angry that his son was taking off for the night without permission. "At least Nikki didn't pull the trigger."

"You still got the scars on your ass?"

"Been a while since I checked."

And there was the awkwardness. Jericho was pretty sure he must have been *trying* to bring the conversation here, because he hadn't needed to mention the gun, and had known what memory it would call up for Wade. It had been inevitable that they'd both remember that summer night in the woods, two teenagers laughing and full of adrenaline, Jericho shucking his buckshot-torn jeans to check for damage, Wade searching Jericho's skin for bits of shot, by flashlight and by touch . . . and everything that had happened after that. Two wild boys, first aid that had turned into wrestling and then into groping and grinding, hungry mouths finding sustenance of a whole new kind—

Jericho sipped his drink, only willpower keeping him from gulping it. Yeah, for whatever reason, he'd been the one to bring the conversation in that direction. So now he should be the one to get it back on track. "I just need to make sure my father's widow and kids are okay. Make sure they're safe. Once I've got that under control, I'm done. I'm gone."

"Well, I'm not sure that's much of an incentive, Jay. I help you with your little chore, and then I'm deprived of your company?"

"I didn't come here to ask for your help."

"Why *did* you come here, then? What was your plan? You thought I was the one behind whatever happened to poor Nikki, so you were going to talk me out of going back for more? Ask a favor for old times' sake? Or was I supposed to be so intimidated by your manliness that I rolled over and gave up?"

All those options sounded pretty ridiculous, Jericho had to admit. "I guess I was hoping you'd just tell me what you wanted, and I'd see if there was some way to get it to you."

"That's practical, isn't it? I thought Jericho Crewe was a man with moral standards. I thought he believed in doing what was right, not what was easy?"

"The Jericho Crewe you knew wasn't a man at all. He was a boy. And he was full of shit most of the time."

Wade nodded slowly. "Yeah. I suppose he was." His gaze was sweet but sharp as he added, "I always liked that about him."

Jericho tried to recover his composure after the heat in that look. "Well, I'm sorry to disappoint you, but I've gotten older, and I've got a lot less energy for crusades. I want to do what I have to do in order to go home with a clean conscience. That's it."

"Even if what you have to do is something illegal?"

"I've done illegal things before, Wade. You know that."

"You've broken the laws of man, sure. But you never broke the Laws of Jericho."

Jericho snorted. He'd forgotten about those. "Wasn't one of the laws, 'Thou shalt not bogart the doobage'?"

"Well? *Do* you bogart the doobage?"

"I'm a police officer, Wade. I don't smoke up anymore."

"That's still obeying your law. Not smoking at all definitely falls inside the not bogarting rule." Wade thought for a moment, then added, "And wasn't one of your rules about being real? Not being a hypocrite? There are plenty of cops who smoke weed, you know. But not you, because you don't want to bust someone else for doing something you do yourself. Right?"

Jericho was too tired to talk to Wade. It was too hard to keep his defenses up, and too frightening to even think about letting them down. There was a time they could have been quiet together. A time Wade would have understood what Jericho needed, and given it to him. But that time was gone, so Jericho carefully set his glass on the corner of the desk and stood up. "I'm not sure what I'm doing here," he admitted. "It made sense when I thought of it, I guess. And it was good to see you again, Wade."

"I don't know why you're making it sound like good-bye, Jay." Wade was still sitting down, and he looked up at Jericho with a beatific smile. "You said you were planning to stay in Mosely until Nikki and the kids were out of trouble?" He sipped his bourbon and his eyes were quicksilver gray. "If that's what you're waiting for, Jay? You better get comfortable. You're going to be in Mosely for a long damn time."

CHAPTER 4

Jericho left the SUV in the bar parking lot. He was a big man and hadn't had that much to drink, but he wanted to clear his head anyway. And he'd get a better feel for the town on foot than behind the wheel.

Not that he needed to spend much time reacquainting himself with Mosely. Now that he'd gotten over his adjustment to the size of the place, he was finding that little had changed. Maybe the houses were a bit more raggedy than they'd been before he left, but the difference was too subtle to be sure it wasn't just another illusion brought about by the contrast with LA's sprawling newness. Mosely was Mosely, just as it had always been.

Jericho walked through the backstreets for a few blocks, then came back out on the main drag and on a whim ducked into the hardware store. He'd worked there on and off during his teens, doing whatever grunt work Mr. Appleby, the store owner, didn't want to handle. Jericho braced himself now to see someone else behind the battered wooden counter, but somehow wasn't surprised to see a familiar, if older, face.

"Mr. Appleby," he said.

"Jericho. Good to see you." A casual nod, as if Jericho had been gone for a week or two, then Mr. Appleby set down the calculator he'd been holding and stepped out from behind the counter. "Sorry about your father. He was an asshole, but family's family."

Jericho snorted. "That boils it down pretty well."

"My Mary always says I have a way with words."

"Is Mrs. Appleby doing okay?"

"She's as good as can be expected. We're both getting on, naturally."

Another pithy truth. Jericho figured he might as well take advantage of the old man's forthrightness. The hardware store had always been a place to exchange gossip, and Mr. Appleby was an avid listener and collector of information. "You don't know who my father would have been mixed up with, do you? I mean, what sort of business he might have been doing?"

A raised eyebrow. "I think everyone knows what *sort* of business he was doing." Mr. Appleby shrugged. "But with who? That's a bit more complicated. Wade, of course. Not much goes on around here, at least on the shady side, that Wade's not a part of. You seen him yet?" There was an overly bright tone to the question that made it clear Jericho was expected to give a little gossip if he wanted any in return.

"Just came from the bar. He seems to be doing all right for himself."

"He's a survivor."

"I guess so. And he's the only one of my father's business partners you can think of?"

"The only one I could call by name, I think. There's a few other characters around town, but something like this? I heard the police were investigating it as a murder. That true?"

"I'm not getting a lot of information from them, but it seems that way, yeah."

Mr. Appleby shook his head, and then turned his attention to a man wearing a green store apron shuffling down the aisle toward them. "Will," Mr. Appleby called. "You okay?"

The man lifted his head, and Jericho squinted at him.

"Will Archer?" Jericho took a half step closer. They'd gone to school together, he was sure of it. "Will? It's Jericho Crewe."

An unreadable look, and then the man turned to Mr. Appleby, ignoring Jericho entirely.

"What do you always do if you haven't got another job?" Mr. Appleby prompted gently, and after a moment, Will turned and headed toward the broom that was leaning against the wall by the storeroom door. "Good work, Will. Thank you."

Mr. Appleby's voice was only a little lower when he told Jericho, "Car accident, about eight years ago now. Drunk driver hit him head on and scrambled his brain pretty bad. He was working here already, managing the place while Mary and I got ready to retire.

Didn't seem fair to let him go, even if he's not as quick as he used to be."

Jericho watched the man painstakingly sweep the clean floor. "But he's not the manager anymore?" No, of course he wasn't. Mr. Appleby had put off his own retirement in order to come back and run the place. He'd changed his life's path in order to help someone else stay closer to his.

Mr. Appleby shrugged. "We were talking about your father's death, weren't we? Honestly, I'm not sure who else might have been involved. I don't see any of our local boys getting into anything quite that... ambitious. Maybe the Mountaineers? I'm never sure whether they're just trying to live up to the biker reputation or if they really are as bad as they seem. Sam Tennant and his militia types? I'd say they're in the same category—they talk a good game, but they don't do much as far as I've heard. Your old friend Kayla Morgan might be able to tell you a bit more about both of those groups."

Another quick glance, clearly trying to find a reaction to Kayla's name, then another shrug. "From what I've seen personally, though? I'd think Wade was your best bet. I'm not saying he's disposed toward violence, necessarily. But he does what has to be done, and in his line of work? Sometimes things get rough, as I understand it."

Jericho hadn't asked Wade about Eli's death, not specifically. He hadn't wanted to know, and he realized that he still didn't. "I'm looking for information on events *after* my father's death. Sounds like somebody's been harassing his wife. I thought it might be connected to the murder, but it could be totally separate too."

"Harassing a widow? Well, that opens things up a good ways. We have lots of small-time assholes who might pull crap like that."

"Yeah, I figured."

"She okay? She's a tough one; if it was worth her complaining about, it was probably pretty bad."

"She's not hurt. But shook up, I'd say. Especially with the kids to worry about."

Mr. Appleby nodded. "Yeah. She's a bit—a bit hard, from what I've seen. But I do truly believe she loves those kids."

"They seem like they're kind of wild. I mean, I don't know much about kids, but..."

Mr. Appleby raised an eyebrow. "I'd say kids running wild is a tradition in that house. And you turned out okay, eventually."

"Took me a while. And I had some outside help." He smiled and nodded around the hardware store. "I asked a lot of people in this town for a job before you gave me a chance. I've always really appreciated you letting me work here."

"Now, I don't think you *always* appreciated it. Not when you had to unload the morning deliveries all by yourself, you didn't."

Jericho grinned. "Sure, there were some details I could have done without. But overall? Thank you."

Mr. Appleby waved the words away, and they made small talk for a while, that low-level information exchange that was right on the edge between sharing news and gossiping. Then they shook hands, Jericho sent his best wishes along to Mrs. Appleby, and he headed back out to the street. He said good-bye to Will on the way, but was ignored.

Was there any point in continuing his tour? It gave him something to do. If he wasn't doing this, he'd have to go back out to the house and deal with Nikki, and he wasn't quite ready for that yet. It was just so *strange*, seeing her there in that house, especially with the kids running around. Strange to *not* see his father.

And to know that he would never see his father again. It was over. Whatever had been left unsaid would never *be* said. But what would Jericho have wanted to say, anyhow? Or to hear?

He got a few surprised looks from people who seemed to recognize him as he strolled through downtown. Some of them he remembered, others he didn't, but none of them inspired him to stop walking and start talking. He hadn't had many friends in Mosely, or anywhere else for that matter. He'd been a loner, until he, Kayla and Wade had formed their unlikely triumvirate.

Jericho had made it to the south end of town, turned around and crossed the street, and was halfway back to the bar when a dark sedan pulled up to the curb in front of him. He wasn't exactly shocked when two dark-suited men climbed out of the front seats.

"Special Agent Hockley. Almost-as-Special Agent Montgomery. Nice to see you both again."

"Detective Crewe. Or just *Mister* Crewe, right? Since you're on vacation."

"The DEA not doing any of that sensitivity training these days? I'm here to bury my father, Agent Montgomery, not to appreciate the scenery."

Montgomery managed to look abashed, but Hockley was undeterred. "We don't see that many pedestrians in Mosely. People mostly drive to where they're going. Mind telling us where you left your car?"

"It's up the road a bit. I appreciate your enthusiasm for the whole serve-and-protect thing, but I'm pretty fit. I can make it back without any trouble. Was there anything else you wanted to talk about? Maybe we could discuss your investigation into my father's murder?"

"That isn't your rental in the parking lot at Wade Granger's bar, is it?"

"Is that Wade's bar?"

Agent Hockley stepped closer, obviously trying to be menacing. "You know whose bar it is. And you were specifically told to stay away from Mr. Granger. Is there a reason you ignored that instruction?"

"A reason?" Jericho shrugged. "Not really. No reason to ignore it, but no reason to pay attention to it, either. So ignoring it seemed like a reasonable default." He gave Hockley his best shit-eating grin, the one that used to drive Deputy Garron and Kayla's dad into quiet rages, the one he hadn't bothered to use for years now. There was just something about being back in Mosely that brought it out in him, he supposed. "Hey, can you give me any suggestions for other people I should be talking to? I'm trying to get my father's affairs in order, as one does after a death, and it seems like his affairs were a bit— Well, I'm not sure how I'd characterize them. Agent Montgomery, you've got a way with words. How would *you* characterize my father's affairs?"

Montgomery squinted at him, but it was Hockley who said, "Detective Crewe, you are a private citizen in this jurisdiction. As such, you have no special obligations to follow our instructions. But may I remind you that you are *not* a private citizen at home, and the DEA works quite closely with the Los Angeles Police Department on many issues of mutual concern. We have contacts in LA, and friends. Powerful friends. It will not be good for your career *there* if you continue to be a nuisance *here*. Have I made myself clear?"

Jericho bit back the quick retort. He wasn't worried about the threat to his job, but the agent's words had been a good reminder that he and Hockley were, in the big picture view, on the same side. Jericho's instinct was defiance, but he should make sure he was challenging authority for a reason, not just because returning to his old stomping grounds had made him revert to his punk-kid persona. As annoying as Hockley was, he wasn't completely wrong in his goals. It was textbook police work to try to keep a civilian away from an active investigation, especially if the civilian was related to the victim. Hockley's refusal to make an exception in Jericho's case was irritating, but not inappropriate. "You have made yourself clear," he confirmed. No promises, just a refusal to get into the pissing match Hockley seemed to be looking for. "Is there anything else you wanted to discuss?"

Hockley paused, as if running over a mental checklist. Or maybe savoring his little power trip—Jericho might understand the guy's motives, but that didn't mean he had to appreciate his attitude. "I think that's all for now," the agent finally said. Jericho had delivered a similar message in the past, but he hadn't been such a prissy bastard when he'd done it.

Jericho nodded. "Okay, then. It's been nice chatting, but I'd better get going. I don't want to miss happy hour at Wade's bar."

He started walking. The last shot had been stupid and petty, but it had felt good. And after all the confusion of the day, just feeling good was pretty damn important.

CHAPTER 5

Despite his bravado, Jericho didn't go back inside the bar when he picked up his rental. It wasn't that he was worried about what the agents would say or do, but he didn't want to run into Wade again. Not yet.

Going back out to the house didn't appeal, either, but Jericho didn't see a choice. He couldn't go home until he had things sorted out with Nikki, and he couldn't sort things out without getting more information from her. He'd believed Wade when he'd said he had nothing to do with whoever had shown up at the house, so he needed to know who *else* Eli had been doing business with. And his limited inquiries with Wade and Mr. Appleby had done him no good.

He sat there behind the wheel in the parking lot, his mind worrying over it all like a tongue probing at a set of broken teeth. His father was dead. Dead. Eli Crewe was no longer a force in Jericho's life. But the mess he'd created, the mess that had killed him, was still oozing over the people he'd left behind.

After a few useless minutes, a man in a dark suit, white shirt, and dark tie approached, and Jericho wasn't sorry when the concrete matter of wardrobe choices distracted him from more nebulous concerns. There might be a reason for a man to be dressed this conservatively in Mosely, Montana, but he couldn't think of what it might be, other than the obvious. The guy's look wasn't quite aggressive enough for Homeland Security. Not nerdy enough for DEA. Jericho rolled his window down as the man arrived beside the car, and said, "FBI?"

The man grinned at him, dimples flashing. "They *said* you were a detective—guess they were right." He reached into his breast pocket and pulled out an ID anyway, then said, "Dean Lachey. Okay if we talk for a minute?"

"Yeah, okay." Jericho wasn't sure whether he should be bracing himself for when the trap was sprung, but he couldn't really refuse such a legitimate, polite request. What was he going to say, he was too busy staring into space to talk to a federal officer?

Lachey took a couple of steps at a jog as he headed around the front of the rental as if reluctant to keep Jericho waiting. It might have been a good idea to look at the ID a little more closely, because this guy was acting like no fed Jericho had ever worked with. Still, it was broad daylight in a public space—there was nothing to be afraid of.

And when Lachey had found his seat, he smiled again and it was pretty much impossible to see a threat. If Jericho wasn't careful, he might even start seeing something else, like how boyishly handsome the agent was, how well his shoulders filled out the suit jacket—no. *Bad brain. Not appropriate.*

"What can I help you with?" Jericho asked, and did *not* think of how that line would fit into a porn movie.

"I was just hoping to get some background, if that's okay. I know you already met with our DEA colleagues, but—" another easy smile "—based on the transcripts I saw of that conversation, I think their charm was as effective with you as it is with everyone else."

"So you're here to charm me?" Jericho raised an eyebrow. "I guess I should be flattered, but I'm not sure what I've done to deserve the effort."

"The FBI believes in taking a holistic approach. DEA's been in town for way too long to have come up with as little as they have—they're starting to get desperate. FBI's got a few other irons in the fire up here, and our higher-ups aren't pushing as hard. We're happy to take a few notes on people who are bit players, or who aren't playing at all, and add them to our file. We don't need to try to turn you into some sort of master villain."

"That's reassuring. So—what do you need to know?"

"I've got the basic information from the file the DEA are building. I'm mostly interested in anything you've discovered *since* you met with them. You've been out to the house, as I understand it?"

And for the first time, Jericho felt a hint of sharpness behind the other man's casual demeanor. "You have the house under surveillance?" he asked. "Or . . . you have *me* under surveillance? How did you know I'd been out there?"

"'Surveillance' is a generous term. You were seen heading out of town toward the house, that's all. The rest was a guess. But it was a good guess, right?"

"It was a good guess," Jericho conceded. "So, yes, I was out there."

"You met with Nikki Crewe," Lachey prompted.

"I did."

"And did she give you any information you think might be relevant to the investigation of your father's death?"

"She may have, yeah. I'm only starting to get a feel for the situation . . ."

Lachey nodded encouragingly.

"She said she thought Eli was killed because of something he had. She says she doesn't know what it is, says she's searched the house and can't find anything."

"So it's in the house? It wasn't on the body or taken by the perp?"

"She doesn't know. Says some goons came out and tried to scare her into giving it to them, but she has no idea what they were looking for."

"That's a lot of 'she says' for one story. You don't believe her?"

"I don't believe or disbelieve. Like I said, I'm only starting to get a feel for what's going on. Her story seems plausible, and I don't have another explanation."

"And she has *no idea* what the 'goons' were looking for or where it might be? She didn't have any idea who they were or who'd sent them?"

"That's what she says." Jericho frowned as he recognized his reluctance to say any more. His good sense took over, luckily, and he made himself add, "Well, she speculated that Wade Granger might be involved. That's why I was here at the bar. But she didn't have real evidence, and he didn't say anything incriminating. Denied all knowledge of the situation."

"And you believed him?"

Yeah, Jericho had believed him. But he couldn't back that feeling up with much beyond wishful thinking and basic instincts, so he shrugged. "Same category as Nikki. I'm just telling you what he said."

"You think Nikki's going to tell you more? I've never questioned her myself, but the story around the station is that she's just as stubborn and uncooperative as her—" Lachey caught himself, then seemed to realize he'd already said too much to avoid continuing "—as your father." He paused as if waiting for Jericho to take offense, but there was absolutely nothing about the statement that could be contradicted. *Stubborn* and *uncooperative* were mild descriptors for Eli Crewe. Finally Lachey went on. "Do you get the feeling she's thinking of you as an ally? You think she might open up to you about any of this?"

"I get the feeling she's thinking of me as a tool. In pretty much all meanings of the word. She'll tell me more if she decides it's in her best interest to tell me more." He thought back to the scene in the kitchen and added, "Or the kids' best interests. But I assume those would be the same as hers."

Lachey nodded, then slid his hand into his jacket pocket and pulled out a business card. "Here's how to reach me. If she says anything you think might be useful, I'd appreciate a heads-up. We're all on the same side here, after all. The brotherhood of law enforcement, right?"

It was fairly rare to hear a fed acknowledge much kinship with anyone but other feds, at least in Jericho's experience, but he didn't bring that up. He took the card, exchanged a handshake made somewhat awkward by their positions in the car, and then watched Lachey climb out and return to his vehicle.

He probably should have asked a few more questions. Possibly a *lot* more questions if he wanted to find out what had happened to his father and who was responsible. But he wasn't sure he *did* want to find out about that. Maybe it was easier to not know, and maybe trying to solve this problem with Nikki was the distraction he needed. So he drove back to the house feeling a bit lighter, a bit calmer.

He pulled up near the rough front steps and saw Elijah and Nicolette over by the woodpile, at the feet of an adult-sized yellow mountain bike that looked well used but also cared for, unlike the house itself. The kids were playing some sort of game with the wood chips. Playing or fighting—it wasn't completely clear, and Jericho didn't want to get involved enough to make it any clearer. He'd never liked kids that much, not until they were old enough to start making sense and to show at least a little self-control. When they were young and crazy, like Elijah and Nicolette obviously were, the best policy was to stay the hell away from them and hope someone responsible came along to keep them in line. That had worked for him in LA, and hopefully it would keep working for him here.

So he parked the SUV and kept his face turned toward the house. He heard Nicolette screaming some language that would probably get her kicked out of most schools in the country, and tried not to wince. If he acknowledged that he'd heard, he might be expected to do something about it.

But there was Nikki, standing inside the screen door watching the kids, and she was clearly not inspired to go out and deal with them, so maybe Jericho didn't have to worry about his inaction. "They carry on like that a lot?" he asked.

"Their father just died." Nikki stared at him like he was a snake she was about to hit with a shovel. "You think this is the best time for an etiquette lesson?"

Jericho didn't point out that Nicolette was using the obscenities like they were old friends, not recent acquaintances. It wasn't any of his business. "I went to see Wade. He says he had nothing to do with the guys who came by."

"And you believe him." Nikki nodded cynically. "Eli always said you were a bit slow."

Fast enough to get out of this shithole. But there was no point starting that fight. If Nikki did have more information than she was sharing, as Lachey clearly suspected, Jericho needed to keep the peace. All the same, maybe he could use the insult as a way into the conversation he wanted to have.

"If I'm so slow, why'd you call me? And why'd you tell me to come quick, as if there'd be something I could do if I got here soon enough?" He leaned against the post that held up the porch roof and squinted at her. *"You really think Eli would marry an innocent woman, Jay?"* "What was the plan, Nikki? Why did you want me here if you thought I'd be useless?"

"I can think something will be true and still hope it might not be." She looked past him, out to the squabbling children. "And Eli said you and Wade were close, back in the day." She looked toward him as if to see his reaction when she added, "Eli said you were *real* close."

Was he supposed to be upset by that little dig? If Nikki thought he was worried about being outed, she should think again. Wade, on the other hand—Jericho had no idea how Wade would feel about it. Being gay in LA was one thing, but being gay in Mosely was probably quite another. It had certainly been a big deal back when Jericho had lived there; both he and Wade had been aware of the chances they were taking every time they were together, but it had somehow made each encounter even hotter. And who knew if Wade even *was* gay, or whether fooling around with Jericho had been just one more random experience, one more wild adventure, for a man who'd try anything once and take any dare he was offered.

Still, there was no need to pay attention to Nikki's innuendo. "So you thought I could use an old friendship with Wade to—what? What are you hoping for, here?"

"Your father wouldn't have needed me to *tell* him how to handle this."

"My father's way of handling 'this' is likely what got him killed. So I think I want to take a different path. And I honestly have no real idea what 'this' is. Some goons are looking for something they think Eli had. Chances are pretty good they killed him in order to get it. You say you've looked around for whatever it is and haven't found it. Do you have *any* idea what it might be?"

"I *told* you: I figured it was drugs or guns. If it's not that, I have no clue."

Jericho sighed. Maybe she really didn't know anything, and even if she was lying, he wasn't going to have much luck bullying the truth out of her, not if the feds had already tried and failed. He needed a different approach. "What's the plan for you guys, now? Do you have somewhere you could go? Do you have a job you have to worry about? Have you got family you could go stay with? Maybe start again somewhere new? I can stick around for a couple days, but I'm not going to be your permanent bodyguard. We need a longer-term solution, and if you can't give these guys what they want, maybe you just need to get the hell away from the situation."

"Yeah, Eli *said* you were a quitter."

Jericho thought wistfully of his simple life back in LA. "I guess I'm not going to be too helpful, then. You've heard my best suggestions, and you don't like them. You don't have any better ideas, or if you do, you won't share them with me. So I think I'm done here." He refused to consider his duty toward the kids, who seemed to have stopped fighting and were now sprawled in the dirt staring up at the sky. Possibly they'd knocked each other out, but that wasn't his problem. None of this was his problem. "Good luck with it. Let me know when the funeral is and I'll send flowers."

"You think I have *money* for going somewhere and starting over?" Nikki hissed, stalking forward. "You think I'd be living in this shithole for one more goddamn second if I had a fucking *choice*?"

Damn. Another familiar dynamic. The anger to cover vulnerability, the aggression to disguise fear. There went his quick escape. "How much money would you need? I could probably loan you some—enough to get you set up somewhere temporary until this place sold and you could go more permanent. I don't expect Eli had any life insurance?"

She snorted. "No. No insurance. For the rest—I'd need enough for moving expenses, and for rent and groceries. And it could be a while before this house sells, and even when it does I'm not going to get all that much for it."

"Let's be clear here: I'm talking about a loan. A few grand, maybe, enough to get you moved and cover the first month's rent. But you'll need to get a job. I'm not planning to keep paying for you forever. And don't start on how Eli always said I was cheap, or how he would have provided for you better. 'Cause I'm not Eli, and I'm not looking to turn into him."

She scowled at him. "Well, then, I guess I can't afford to leave. I need to stick around and try to work out what those guys were searching for. If they want it so bad, maybe I can use it."

"It seems like they wanted it bad enough to kill Eli for it." Unless Eli had pissed off someone in a completely different way, which was certainly possible. "Is that a chance you want to be taking?"

"I have two kids to provide for. I'll do what it takes."

"Even if it takes getting a job and working to give them a normal life?" He frowned then. "Wait a second. It's Tuesday. Why weren't they in school today?"

"Their father died yesterday! They're *grieving*."

Jericho refused to look over and see what form the kids' grieving was taking at that moment. Did they even know about Eli's death? They sure didn't seem too upset about it. Then again, he probably didn't seem too upset either. "Fine. So this is up to you. If you want me to go visit some more people and try to find out what the goons are searching for, I can do that, but you'll have to give me some names. If you want me to contact the local police again to get them investigating this side of the case, I can do that. If you want to get the hell out of here, I can help set something up that way. What's the next step, Nikki?"

"I can't go anywhere until I get the truck. You're a cop; you know how they work. Can you get the truck back for me?"

"I doubt it," Jericho admitted. He supposed Eli had always *said* he was useless. "I don't have much pull in Mosely. And even in LA, if they think it has evidence in it, they'll keep it until the crime lab gets through with it. I can check in, make sure they know you need it, but I doubt it'll do much good."

Nikki tilted her head. "You sure? Eli said you were pretty damn tight with Kayla Morgan too, back in the day. You don't think she'd want to help out an old *friend*?"

"Sure, I expect she'd want to," he said, ignoring the innuendo. How much had Eli known about his son's sexual activities anyway? "But wanting to help a friend isn't enough of a reason to compromise a murder investigation. Especially not one the feds are poking around in."

"The feds?" Nikki's eyes widened. "Are the feds in charge of this? Why?"

"I don't know if they're in charge, but they're certainly involved." He watched her more closely. "What can you tell me about Eli's business? If he was running drugs across the border, that'd be DEA for sure. If he was doing anything across state lines, that could get the FBI involved. And god knows Homeland Security pokes their snotty little noses in anywhere they feel like."

She shook her head tiredly. "Well if the feds are involved, I can't run away, can I? Where'm I going to go to get away from *them*?"

"Wait. It wasn't the feds who sent goons to smash up your stuff, Nikki. They're the good guys." More or less. "But if they're involved, it might mean that whoever's messing with you is someone pretty serious. You wouldn't be leaving to get away from the feds, just from whoever else is causing you trouble. So maybe it's time to go?"

She looked over toward the kids, then back at Jericho. "Yeah. Maybe. You could help with that?"

"What would you need?"

"Money. Transportation. And time. I need to wrap a few things up here. I'm not going to sneak away like you did. I need to say good-bye. Collect some debts, pay some debts. Tidy up. You know?"

"What kind of 'debts' are you talking about?"

"I got a paycheck coming to me for a bit of work I did. And they let me run an account at the grocery store, 'cause they trust me to pay it back when I can. *Those* kind of debts."

"Okay. So a couple hours?"

"Maybe a couple days. Everything takes longer than you think it will. And I need to make sure Eli's seen to right; I owe him that. So we could leave after the funeral."

"That's quite a while. It gives whoever's after you a lot of chances to get back out here and take another shot."

"Well, if they try, they'll have a treat waiting for them, won't they? Now that I know they're coming, I'll be ready with the Remington. And there's a little added fun from LA's finest. You *do* have a gun, don't you? And you're a good size. You surprised me when you came in this morning. I didn't recognize you. Eli had some pictures, but only from when you were a kid. I guess I figured you'd have the same build as Eli, but you're a good bit taller, and wider in the shoulders. And you were a Marine? So you can fight?"

"If I have to. But I don't want to do it in a house with two sleeping kids. If you're staying in town, that doesn't mean you have to stay *here*. I'll put you all up at a motel, okay? That'll be safer."

"You think so? 'Cause there's only one motel in town, and it's not exactly a fortress. Everyone would know where we were. And that'd leave *this* place undefended, for those bastards to come in and tear apart." She frowned. "No. This is my home, and they can't fucking have it, not until I'm ready to give it up. The kids can stay with friends. There's a family down the road with kids they go to school with. The mom's a bitch, but she's working real hard to be a pillar of the fucking community. She'll take them in for a couple nights just so she can feel superior about having done it."

Jericho reluctantly smiled. He knew the kind of woman Nikki was talking about. He'd probably been babysat by a few of them when he was little. "That's a good idea. And then, yeah, okay. I can stay here. Help you keep an eye on the place. But I want to call the cops and let them know what's up. Maybe they won't do anything, but maybe they will, and if someone ends up shot, I want to be able to say we did everything right leading up to it."

She nodded, although she didn't look pleased. "Okay. But just the regular cops, not the feds. And they do *not* have my permission to search the place. No way."

It was a start. So Jericho called the sheriff's office from the long-corded kitchen phone and took the handset outside before he left a message on Kayla's voice mail. He tried to make it clear that the situation was serious without sounding like he was telling her how to do her job. A fine balance, and one he probably didn't pull off. It was hard to think of quiet Kayla as the sheriff; she likely had a similar problem with thinking of rebellious Jericho as a detective. He thought about calling Lachey and decided against it; he had nothing to report, and he'd be damned if he'd undermine the authority of an old friend just because a fed had been civil to him for a change.

He knocked on the screen door when he was done with the call, then stuck his head inside the kitchen and said, "It's me. Don't shoot."

"You're safe for now," Nikki replied. She was in the kitchen, peering into the fridge. "Any chance I could borrow your truck? I can drop the kids off at the Mastersons', then go into town and run a few errands. Take care of some of the stuff I need to, and pick up groceries while I'm at it."

Jericho tried to remember the details of his car rental agreement, but couldn't. "Why don't I drive you? Safer for you to be with someone, and I'm not sure if other people are allowed to drive the rental."

"That'd leave the house empty. I don't want to make it too easy for them. And I'll be fine in town—there's lots of people keeping an eye on me. Not like I'm going to get jumped at the grocery store in broad daylight."

"Maybe *I* won't be safe out here."

"I'll try to make it back before it gets too late, so I can protect you." She smiled, then stood in front of him expectantly. "Keys?"

He gave them to her. He had no idea when he'd turned into such a pushover.

Ten minutes later he watched as the SUV sped off down the lane, the kids bouncing around in the backseat with no sign of seat belts. They'd been excited about the chance to ride in the rental, excited about spending the night in the fancy house down the road. Jericho hadn't realized how much he'd forgotten about growing up poor until he saw their reactions to stuff he'd learned to take for granted.

But now they were gone, and he was alone in the house.

This was what he'd been expecting that morning when he'd driven out from town. He'd spend some time in the place, getting used to the idea of it being empty, without his father. He'd have the chance to say good-bye, not so much to the person, but to everything *associated* with the person.

He slowly climbed the stairs and peeked into his old bedroom. It was clearly Elijah's space now, with a little boy's clothes and toys scattered all over the floor, a mess that never would have been tolerated when Jericho had lived there. Had Nikki been better at deflecting Eli's rages than Jericho's own mother, or had the old bastard just mellowed with time? Then he stepped inside, around a pile of plastic dinosaurs, and sat gently on the side of the bed. Most of the furniture was the same, and maybe it was even the same mattress.

He poked doubtfully at the tangled sheets and blankets, then shoved them aside and lay down flat, gazing up at the ceiling that had once been so familiar. Flashes of memory came to him: his mother in this room, sweeping his hair back off his face as she soothed him to sleep. Later, the dark comfort of the space between the bed and the wall where he'd hidden after her funeral, unable to face his father or the rest of the world without her sweet protection. And long after that, the hole he'd punched in the plaster—he looked over at the Transformers poster and heaved himself to his feet, lifting a corner to see the jagged gap still there. He'd been angry about—he couldn't remember what, now. But it had been the first time he'd let himself express his frustration with anything but tears. It had felt good, punching the wall, as if his temper was evidence that he was becoming a man—becoming like his father. It had taken him several years of military discipline to learn that true manhood came from maintaining control, not losing it.

He sat back down on the bed and waited, though he wasn't sure for what. A release of some sort? For the world to stop spinning quite so damn quickly? He'd kept his cool through the whole day, even after learning about his father's death and the family he hadn't known he had. But surely he could let his guard down now. He was alone, he had some time. He could let himself feel.

He made himself think about the good times with his father; they must have existed. The old man teaching the son to shoot—that was a Hallmark moment, at least for Redneck Hallmark. But Eli had been half-drunk when he'd taken Jericho out into the backyard and handed him a .30-06. He'd laughed when Jericho had stumbled backward and cried out at the recoil after his first shot, laughed again when Jericho had summoned his courage, tucked the stock in tighter to his shoulder, and pulled the trigger again, his flinch sending the bullet far from the target. The third shot had brought a satisfying *clink*, though, and Jericho had looked over at his dad, hoping—no, actually *expecting*—to finally see approval on the bastard's face. But Eli had just grunted something about how anyone who wasn't blind could hit a tin can from that close, and told Jericho to stop wasting ammunition on target shooting.

So the only real emotion Jericho could drag up was regret. He wished he'd stuck around Mosely long enough to have at least one knock-down, drag-out fight with the old bastard, one chance to feel the satisfaction of his fist connecting with the old man's—

He stopped himself. His father was dead. He needed to let go of the past. Eli Crewe. What else was there for him to remember about Eli Crewe? The stubborn, angry bastard. He'd barely tolerated Jericho's decision to join the Marines, though it wasn't like Jericho had asked for permission. He'd called home when he finished boot camp to tell Eli where he was and had been told he was an idiot for signing his life away. At the time, bridling under the mindless military discipline, Jericho had been sure his father was right.

But he'd gotten used to the military, eventually. He'd never made it back to Mosely on any of his leaves, but he'd kept in touch with the old man. A fragile truce had been established, one that was shattered when Jericho left the service and signed on with the LAPD.

Jericho walked down to the kitchen and stared at the old-fashioned corded phone that still hung on the wall. He tried to imagine the scene: his father had hung up pretty quick after Jericho told him about his new career path, but what had he done then? Smashed something? Jericho looked around. There was a calendar on the wall, but when he lifted it, he found no hole in the wallboard.

Maybe his father hadn't reacted at all. When Jericho had shared the news, Eli had said that no son of his would ever be a cop, Jericho had disagreed, and Eli had said "No. You're not my son anymore." Then he'd hung up. Apparently he'd meant it. There was no point smashing your house over some random guy becoming a cop. It sure hadn't mattered enough for Eli to get in touch with Jericho again.

Of course, Jericho had never contacted Eli, either. The split had been mutual, possibly the only thing the two of them had ever managed to agree on.

So this final division? It shouldn't be that big of a deal. It *wasn't* that big of a deal. Jericho had lost any chance to resolve anything, but there'd been little to resolve.

Jericho went to find his running gear in the bag he'd hauled out of the SUV before Nikki left. He'd told her he'd stick around the house, but he could still get a good workout in without going too far. And if he pushed himself hard enough, perhaps he'd be able to make his brain turn off for a while. That was all he could ask for right then.

CHAPTER 6

Nikki came back late. By the time she arrived, Jericho had showered in tepid water, played with the water heater for a while without finding the problem, and then eaten cold cereal without milk for dinner. So he wasn't too thrilled to see Nikki come straight from the driver's seat to the front door without reaching into the back of the SUV for anything.

"Where're the groceries?" he asked as she pulled the front door open.

"I'm not your maid, and this ain't a B&B," she growled, and she kept walking, straight past him toward the stairs.

"Hey!" he said, loud and strong enough that she froze on the third step. When she half turned in his direction, he gentled his voice a little. "The keys, please."

"You planning on going somewhere? Now, right before they're most likely to come by?"

"It'd be a hell of lot easier to stay put if you had some damn food in the house, or if you'd brought some back with you. But, no, I'm not planning on going anywhere. I'd just like my keys back."

She stared at him, and for a surreal moment he thought she was going to refuse. If she did, he had no idea what he would do about it; a man could be punched for being an asshole, but a woman was a whole different problem. Was he ready to get physical with a civilian woman? A woman who happened to be his father's widow? No, there was no right way to deal with that situation.

Nikki watched Jericho as he thought it through, at least as far as he got before he stalled. Then she raised her eyebrow and dug the keys out of the front pocket of her jeans. "I might want those back," she said as she tossed them into his outstretched palm.

"I might give them to you," he said, shoving the keys deep into his own pocket. *Not likely.*

"I'm going to get some sleep." She leaned down a little, catching his eye. "We don't have any extra sheets, but there's a blanket down on the couch. You can sleep there."

He wondered what message she was trying to send with the pointed eye contact. Did she honestly think she needed to warn him off? Even if he *had* been straight, he'd hardly be climbing into his father's bed. Had she changed the sheets since the last time Eli had slept in them? "I was thinking I might spend the night in my old room. The bed's not great, but it's longer than the couch."

"I was thinking you'd be on the couch. I'm still thinking that. And since it's my house . . ."

He understood now why she'd wanted to keep the keys: having them in his possession made it pretty tempting to use them. He could get in the SUV and drive back to LA, leaving this mess and this cantankerous woman behind.

Yeah, she should have held on to the keys.

But she was his father's widow, dealing with the man's sudden, violent death, so he supposed he had to cut her some slack. "Yeah, okay. Your house. The couch. Sounds great."

She gave him another unreadable look, then turned and climbed the rest of the way up the stairs. He couldn't tell if she was surprised by his lack of fight or if it was exactly what Eli's assessments had led her to expect. It was nice to realize he didn't really care. He kicked off his shoes, dropped the keys and his phone into one of them and his wallet into the other, unstrapped his shoulder holster, grabbed the somewhat musty-smelling blanket off the back of the couch, and stretched out with his head flat, his calves propped up on the arm. It wasn't comfortable, but he'd definitely slept in worse places. Eight years in the military had made a lot of aspects of civilian life seem pretty easy to take.

He lay there thinking about his old bed upstairs. He and Wade had shared it a few times, when they'd known Eli wouldn't be home. He and Kayla too, but those memories weren't the ones that kept popping into his mind. No, it was Wade who'd made the impression: his hot mouth, his hard body, and the connection between them, the way they'd understood each other and been so sure that no one else ever would.

Jericho wondered if Wade had found someone he could be as close to. As a friend, he supposed he should hope Wade had. It was selfish to want someone else to be lonely just because Jericho was.

Not that he didn't have friends, or bed partners. Nobody serious, though. Maybe he was being naïve to keep searching for the impossible closeness he and Wade had shared. Something that intense? It had burned too hot, and had been too tied up in their mutual confusion and need. Mentally healthy people probably didn't have relationships like that, because you had to be pretty damaged to let someone else that far under your skin. He and Wade had both been raw and exposed, and it had only made sense for them to press themselves together, offering less tender flesh to the outside world. They'd been like newborn puppies, rolling around with their eyes still sealed, with no idea of where one of them started and the other left off. Now that they were grown men and able to take care of themselves, they couldn't be as intimate. Yeah, that was a good explanation.

Leaving Wade behind? Just one more pointless regret that he shouldn't be wasting his energy thinking about.

He drifted off and woke some time later. He was too instantly alert for his return to consciousness to have been natural. Something had woken him. But what?

Acting on instinct, he rolled silently to the floor and reached for his Glock, then scooted forward to slip on his shoes and refill his jeans pockets with all his stuff. The floor creaked overhead, suggesting that Nikki was awake as well. Had she been woken by the same thing that woke him? He waited a few moments, then eased toward the window.

He didn't make it that far. There was a strange *whump* and the sound of shattering glass from the front of the house, the same from the back. A sudden orange glow washed over the windows. *Shit.*

Molotov cocktails. An old wooden house that would burn quickly. Only two doors, both engulfed, and the possibility of shooters outside waiting to finish off anyone who escaped.

It had been years since he'd seen battle, but the old training kicked in. *Control the adrenaline, assess the situation, take action. And protect the civilian.*

"Nikki," he yelled from the bottom of the stairs. The smoke was already stinging his eyes. "You mobile?"

She appeared on the landing, a crouching shadow moving quickly. She had her shoes on and was stuffing something into her pocket. "I'm good. But the bastards set the house on fire!"

"Bathroom window," he said, starting up the stairs. "We need to be fast and careful. They could be out there waiting for us."

Her eyes were wide, but she seemed in control of herself. She headed for the bathroom, and he followed, edging her aside when they reached the window. "Let me go first."

She didn't argue. He slid the window up, scanned for anyone who might be watching for them, then turned and slithered through feetfirst, hanging from the sill for half a second before letting himself fall. It was too easy to imagine the impact of the bullets that would explode into his spine, but none arrived. He landed, found his balance, spun, and searched the tree line for any hostiles. "Clear," he said after a moment. "Come on."

He tilted his head up to see something dangling from the window and reached to catch the familiar stock of his father's Remington. Nikki followed soon after, executing the same hang-and-drop technique Jericho had used. Probably he should have helped her, but he was holding her gun for her, so that was a start. Once she'd landed, fallen to one knee, and then straightened, he tugged on her arm. "Let's go. Head for the trees."

They both sprinted across the patch of rough grass, but there were no shots, not even any shouts, at least none that could be heard over the steadily increasing roar of the fire. When they were safely inside the forest, Jericho turned and searched for any signs of movement, but it seemed like the arsonists were long gone.

Nikki was beside him, her entire body rigid, staring back at the house as if drawing energy from the conflagration. "Those fuckers! They think they can burn me out?"

Jericho didn't bother to say that it wasn't a question of *thinking* they could do it, not with the flames licking up the sides of the building like they were and the closest fire trucks half an hour away. "Do you know who? Did you see anybody?"

"No. I heard a noise from outside, but I didn't want to move the curtain in case they were aiming at the house."

Smart move. Smart decision, one that suggested there was a hell of a lot more to this woman than whatever Jericho had managed to understand thus far.

"You think they're gone?" she demanded. "Does your cell have a signal?"

He dug his phone out to double-check, then shook his head. She apparently didn't have a cell, or had left it in the house, or knew not to bother checking it.

"Have you got your keys?" She was still in take-charge mode, and he was fine with that. "There's usually a cell signal at the top of the hill. We could drive up there, and we'd be able to call the fire department."

He looked over at the growing flames, then back at her.

Her expression was fierce in the dancing orange light. "They might be able to save *something*."

"I'm guessing it wasn't insured?"

She answered the question with a defiant glare. Of course it hadn't been.

"Yeah, okay," he said in response. "Let's see if we can circle around through the trees and get to the car. If we get close, I'll go first, get it started, and open the door for you. You get in and we'll move fast."

He started through the trees, Glock in hand. Trekking through this dark forest, stepping over terrain that had once been as familiar as another child's path from kitchen to TV set. But his childhood travels had never involved burning buildings or anyone more hostile than his father.

He caught a glimpse of a strange shadow ahead and motioned Nikki to stop, not that she likely understood the hand sign. Still, she figured it out and froze, and he crept around to the side until he could be sure it was just an oddly shaped tree branch. Not dangerous, but a good reminder for him to keep his mind on the job.

They reached the truck, which was close enough to the house that he could feel the heat coming off the building in waves, but not so close he had to worry about the vehicle going up in flames. He took a good scan of the area and then a quick look at the SUV. And then another look.

Both tires on the near side were flat. He could only imagine he'd find the same on the far side. Then he noticed the hood raised a bit above flush and realized someone had jimmied it open, probably to mess with the engine. The car was disabled.

"Shit," he growled, and Nikki eased up beside him and saw the damage.

"Were *you* insured?" she asked, a note of vicious satisfaction in her voice.

"I have no idea. Maybe." It wasn't like he'd read the rental agreement too closely. "It's not that far to the neighbors."

"The place down in the valley? It's been empty for three years. No phone there. Closest is the Mastersons."

"Where the kids are?"

"Might as well give the uptight bitch one more reason to feel superior."

Jericho wasn't sure there was anyone in the world snobby enough to feel better about herself because someone else's house had burned down, but he didn't argue.

"Might as well." He looked out at the driveway, then back at Nikki. "You okay staying in the forest for a bit? Are there still trails? I don't think anyone's stuck around to take potshots at us, but I'd rather not be out in the open, just in case."

Nikki nodded. "Yeah. We can make the whole hike off-road."

He stepped back and let her lead the way. It wasn't his forest anymore. But it felt good to be back in it, especially once they got away from the house and he was able to smell the fresh spring forest instead of the smoke. It was full dark, but there was enough moonlight, combined with the flashlight from Jericho's phone, to let them make their way with only occasional stumbles, and the air was cool without being cold. It would have been a nice walk under different circumstances.

And even as it was, Jericho didn't feel too bad. Watching the house burn had been—well, it was a problem for Nikki, of course. And for the kids. Everything they'd owned had just gone up in flames, and it wasn't like it was going to be easy for them to buy it all again. For the family who'd been living in the house, this was a hell of a mess.

But for him, being selfish, it had been a bit cathartic. He'd always had a vague imagining of some final *something* with his father. A showdown or a reconciliation or at least an acknowledgment of past wrongs—a resolution. Something more than an ambiguous phone call from a stranger.

Eli's death had left Jericho feeling cheated, somehow. The old man had been distant while Jericho's mother had been alive, and their relationship had deteriorated quickly after that. He'd pushed young Jericho around, hit him, told him he was useless—the bastard had shot him with buckshot, for Chrissake, and never said a word about it after Jericho had limped home. So watching Eli's house, the site of so much of his cruelty, go up in flames? If it hadn't been for Nikki and the kids, it would have been pretty sweet. Maybe Jericho had never actually won against Eli, but he'd outlasted him, and outlasted his damn house, and that was something. Something that a man who valued toughness as much as Eli had would surely have had to acknowledge as a sort of victory.

Nikki stumbled in front of him, fell to her knees, and made a noise somewhere between a grunt and a sob. Jericho immediately felt like shit. He'd been musing happily about the destruction of her home while she was fighting her way through the forest mourning her second serious loss in a few days. "Want me to take a turn in front?" he asked gently.

"I can do it." She pushed herself to her feet.

"You really don't make it easy to help you."

"You think I need your help just to *walk*?" She scowled at him and started off again.

Jericho followed, and asked, "Why'd you call me in the first place? Why'd you want me to come?"

"You think I shouldn't have told you your father was dead?"

"But you *didn't* tell me he was dead." They'd started moving fast, almost jogging. Maybe Nikki wanted to get away from this conversation. But she hadn't given him a good answer the last time he brought it up, and she wasn't giving him a good answer now. "You told me he was hurt and I needed to come quick. If you'd told me he was dead, I probably wouldn't have come, and you knew that. You *wanted* me to come."

"Yeah, sure. I mean, you've been *so* useful."

Jericho sighed. He was pretty sure Nikki could out-stubborn him without breaking a sweat. So they continued through the forest without talking, covering ground quickly and efficiently. Even so, it was the better part of an hour before the trees around them started to thin and the path widened and became better groomed.

Nikki said, "This is it," as the two of them stepped out onto a manicured lawn. The house sitting in front of them was made to give a rustic impression, all logs and porches and what appeared to be a metal roof, but the place was five times the size of Nikki's house. And despite the late hour, almost every window had a light shining out of it.

"What's going on?" Nikki muttered just loud enough for Jericho to hear. "They having a fucking party?"

The two of them skirted around the pool and Jacuzzi and made their way to the front of the house. Nikki rounded the corner ahead of Jericho and then stopped dead. He had to dodge past her to see what had caught her attention.

There were three Mosely Sheriff's department cruisers in the driveway. Three dark sedans suggested a strong representation of feds as well.

Jericho turned to Nikki and saw her staring at the front door like she was afraid to approach. "Maybe they're investigating the fire," he said, although six cars at a distant neighbor's house seemed like overkill. "And this way we don't have to feel bad about waking them up."

Nikki ignored him, stumbling forward as if she was forcing herself to move. He followed closely.

When they reached the front door, Nikki raised her hand to knock, but the heavy wood moved before she could hit it, opened by Kayla Morgan in her sheriff's uniform. "Jay," she said, sounding relieved. "Mrs. Crewe. We were looking for you. The unit we sent to the house discovered the fire. We were worried you might have been inside."

"We were," Nikki said shortly. "But we decided not to stay. Why'd you send a unit to the house? What's going on?"

"Mrs. Crewe, would you like to come in and sit down?"

"No," Nikki said. Her voice was rising and the tension was beginning to wash off her in waves. "I'd like to see my kids. Where are my kids?"

"We're trying to figure that out, Mrs. Crewe. Please come in and sit down." Kayla stepped aside to give them space, and Jericho caught a glimpse of the scene in the living room: a small cluster of deputies standing around while two adults in pajamas sat on the couch, stunned.

Nikki stepped backward so quickly she ran into Jericho, then jerked forward. "What the fuck are you talking about? I left my kids *here*! I left them here so they'd be safe! Where the fuck are they? Where are my kids?"

Kayla nodded slowly. "I'm sorry, Mrs. Crewe. Apparently some men came to the house. We're gathering evidence now, trying to sort it all out. But there were three or more intruders, and they were armed and wearing masks. They've taken the children."

Kayla kept talking, explaining what the police were doing, but Nikki clearly wasn't hearing any of it. She seemed too lost in the concept, the horrific reality that her children were missing and she didn't know how to get them back.

As Kayla was repeating the standard line about the police doing everything in their power, Nikki whirled toward Jericho. "We need to find them." She sounded fierce, a lioness protecting her young. "They're your brother and sister. Your family. You need to help me. We need to get them back!"

Jericho tried to seem calm and confident. "Of course we will. The police can help too, Nikki."

Nikki cast a disgusted glare in Kayla's direction. "Yeah, I'm sure they'll be *real* helpful." She froze, then turned back to Kayla. "Was it just my kids? They just took mine? Or the Mastersons' too?"

"No, just yours." Kayla was watching Nikki closely. "Can you think of any reason somebody might have wanted to take your children?"

"Maybe the same reason they killed my fucking husband!" Nikki was almost screaming by this point. "But you haven't done shit about that, and you're not going to do shit about this either, are you?"

"We're investigating both crimes," Kayla said. "But we're focusing on this one for now. We'll need to ask you some questions, and the FBI team is setting up at the station as well."

"The FBI?" Nikki snarled. "No. Fuck them! They just want to poke their noses into everything, looking for dirt—"

"Nikki," Jericho said. His voice was louder than he'd planned. "Your kids are missing. They're in trouble. You need to let the FBI help—it's their job. They have experts on this stuff."

She stared at him as if she was trying to read his soul. Trying to decide whether to trust him to guide her through this.

He tried to keep his face impassive. Damn it, he didn't *want* to guide her through it. Didn't want to earn her trust and absolutely didn't want to have to maintain it if she managed to give it to him. He wanted to go back to LA, where the crimes happened to other people and the stricken parents he dealt with were strangers. But those two little kids, wild and fierce and free, in danger because of something they couldn't understand, couldn't control—damn it. Those kids needed their mother to stay strong, and maybe she needed him to help her do that. So he made himself stand straight and wait, and when Nikki's face crumbled and she sagged against him, forcing him to catch her before she fell to the floor, he knew she'd decided. And he knew he was trapped.

CHAPTER 7

Jericho and Kayla managed to work as a loose team, getting Nikki somewhat under control and herding her into the back of a squad car for the trip to the sheriff's station. Jericho climbed in with her because she wouldn't let go of his hand, and as soon as the car door was shut and they were alone, she turned to him and hissed, "The police can't help with this. They won't do what has to be done. This is your family! You need to help us!"

"What are you talking about? The cops have all the tools; they can collect evidence and analyze clues and—"

"*Evidence*?" Nikki squinted at him like she was unsure if he was crazy or just joking. "We don't need any fucking *evidence*. Somebody took *my kids*. I don't want them to have a trial and get sent to fucking *jail*; I want them dead! We need to get the kids back and then we need to take care of whoever took them."

"Let's focus on the first part of that, okay? Let's get the kids back and worry about the rest of it once they're safe."

A deputy climbed into the driver's seat then, cutting the conversation mercifully short. Nikki made the trip to the sheriff's office in silence, although her glare made it obvious she hadn't changed her mind about what needed to happen or what she thought of Jericho's reluctance to join her crusade. When they arrived, they were escorted inside and met by Hockley and Montgomery, neither of whom seemed happy to be renewing their acquaintance.

"Mr. Crewe, if you could come with me, please," Hockley said.

"You're DEA," Jericho responded. "We were expecting FBI."

Nikki looked confused by Jericho's objection, but she straightened up and watched closely, clearly ready to join him in rebelling against any authority she was presented with. He tried to relax his body, sending the message that this wasn't something she needed to get too worried about.

"We're part of a joint task force," Hockley said. "The FBI will focus on the abduction, of course, but until we have evidence to the contrary we're considering this part of a larger situation."

Nikki whirled toward Jericho. "You *see*? They're not interested in getting my kids back! All they care about is whatever they think Eli was doing! They're using this as a way to get into all *that*. They don't care about Elijah and Nicolette."

Shit. Jericho wished Hockley had kept his damn mouth shut. But he'd been responding to an objection Jericho had made, so maybe this was all his own fault. He shook his head and fixed his gaze on Nikki's wide eyes. "It's your kids, Nikki. Whatever they're looking for on top of that? They're searching for the kids too. You need to cooperate with them, tell them whatever you know, because that's how we'll find your children. Nothing else matters, does it?"

She looked like she might argue, but then her face crumbled, and he repeated, "Nothing else matters. We'll find the kids."

Jericho hoped the words weren't a lie. They seemed to calm Nikki, at least, and she let herself be led down the hall to one of the interrogation rooms while Jericho was escorted into another. He sat in a chair, Hockley sat across from him, and Montgomery stood by the door, arms crossed.

"I spoke to your captain in LA," Hockley said once they were settled. "She said you're a good cop. Said you know which rules to respect and which ones can bend a little." Hockley waited, his gaze never leaving Jericho's face. Then he leaned forward. "So I wonder what she'd have to say if she heard you were shacking up with a woman closely associated with the drug trade. I already mentioned the part where you've been drinking with your old friend the notorious criminal. I wonder what she'd think about you interfering with a federal investigation."

"Why don't you give her another call and find out? Then you can stop wondering about stupid crap you're making up for no reason and start worrying about two kidnapped children."

"I'm sorry, are you *denying* that you've been behaving in the ways I've described?"

Jericho sighed. "Let's pretend all that worked, okay? Let's pretend you've got me off-balance and fretting about my career. Let's pretend I'm all softened up and ready to cooperate. So now you can just tell me what you need, I can try to give it to you, and we can get back to what we should be worrying about."

"Why don't you let *me* decide what we should be worrying about?"

Jericho sighed and looked over at Montgomery. "I don't suppose there's any chance you could jump in here, is there? Maybe you could remind your partner that I don't know shit about my father's business, and that we have two missing children to be searching for? We could all think about how important the first twenty-four hours after abduction are? As he pointed out yesterday, we're all on the same fucking side."

Montgomery didn't speak. Hockley leaned back in his chair and tried to stare Jericho down, but after eight years in the Marines, Jericho could keep his gaze locked over someone's shoulder in his sleep. Hockley finally shrugged. "We'll take your statement about the events of this evening, then. Let's start with why you were sleeping at the house, and why whatever you were doing meant the kids needed to be out of the house."

Jericho almost laughed at the insinuation. "Your intel really isn't all that good, huh? You got the official reports but haven't talked to anyone in depth?"

Hockley raised a questioning eyebrow.

But Jericho wasn't going to elaborate on his sexual orientation. Best to stick to the relevant facts. "I stayed at the house because Nikki said there'd been some goons out there making threats. She had the kids sleep at the neighbors' because she thought they'd be safer there. That's all."

"What goons?" Hockley squinted. "She didn't contact the police about that."

"*I* did. I left a message for the sheriff late this afternoon."

"Ah, the sheriff. Another of your old friends."

"And I mentioned it to an FBI agent today too. Agent Lachey—maybe you know him?"

Hockley's squint got just a little tighter, which Jericho wouldn't have thought was possible. "What were the circumstances that led to you contacting Special Agent Lachey?"

"He contacted me," Jericho said. "You'd have to ask *him* about the circumstances that led to it."

"But you didn't see fit to pass this information on to us?"

"You wanted me to let you know the FBI had talked to me?"

"I meant the information about the 'goons.' You didn't tell us about that."

Jericho smiled sweetly. "I guess it slipped my mind."

"And what else has slipped your mind, Mr. Crewe? What other information are you withholding from us?"

"Do you work on Kennedy assassination theories in your spare time? Or are you more into alien cover-ups? Seriously, this much paranoia has *got* to find an outlet somewhere other than in your work." Jericho frowned. "What exactly is it you think I'm involved in? I mean, sleeping with my father's widow—gross, and it didn't happen, but even if it had it wouldn't have been a crime. Having a drink with someone I used to know—also not illegal. Having a conversation with an FBI agent? Fairly acceptable behavior. So what are you getting at with all this?" He suddenly thought of Elijah, leaning out from behind his mother and staring at Jericho with that strange mix of curiosity and fear; there was something bigger than his pride on the line. He sighed and made himself lean back in his chair. "You're right. I'm a cop. I'm on your side. But I honestly have no idea how to help you."

"Why don't you just answer our questions to the best of your ability? *Without* all the bullshit?"

Jericho forced himself to nod. "Okay. Go for it."

Hockley blinked. "Okay." He paused as if gathering his thoughts. "Have you had any contact with your father in the last few years?"

"No."

"Have you had any contact with Wade Granger since you left Mosely?"

"Not until today."

"Contact with any associates of your father or Wade Granger?"

"Not to my knowledge."

"What is your purpose for being in Mosely at this time?"

Well, that one was a bit trickier. "I came here because Nikki called me and said my dad had been in an accident." He left out the part where she hadn't mentioned that he was already dead. Maybe he should have shared the information, but he still didn't really understand what Nikki had been up to with her omissions, and he didn't trust this DEA asshole. "I've stuck around to help Nikki and the kids get settled."

"The kids." Hockley smiled blandly. "What are their names, again?"

Damn. Jericho should have had this ready. "Elijah. And—Nicola—no, Nicolette."

Hockley nodded. "Yeah. You and the kids are real close."

"We're not close. We're family. It's a whole different thing."

Hockley didn't look impressed, but he let it go. He recorded the details of Jericho's evening, asked a few moderately relevant questions for clarification, and then had him sign a copy of the statement.

"Okay," Hockley said when that was all taken care of. "That's it for now. Are you planning to stay in the area, or head home?"

"The kids—my half brother and sister—they're still missing." Why was it so hard for Hockley to understand what that meant? "So I'm planning to stick around until they're safe."

"In the area? Fine. You want to support your 'family'? Sure. But if you're thinking of being part of the investigation?" Hockley shook his head. "No. You need to stay out of this, just like you should have stayed out of it before. This is an official matter, Mr. Crewe. A *federal* matter."

It wasn't worth arguing about. Jericho was escorted out of the interrogation room. He asked about Nikki and was told that she'd be with the investigators for considerably longer, so he left his cell number for her to call him when she got out.

Then he headed down the hallway to the office marked *Sheriff*. The door was open and Kayla was inside, already dull-eyed, staring at her computer screen as if willing it to give her answers she needed.

"You had breakfast yet?" he asked her.

She blinked hard. "Uh, no, I guess not."

"You have half an hour to come eat with me?"

"Apparently I have all day. The feds appreciate the use of my office space and my support staff, but they've got the investigation covered." She kept her tone level and her expression neutral, but it was clear how she felt about being edged out.

"Okay, good. Half an hour seemed a bit stingy for a meal." He waited expectantly until she stood and grabbed her jacket.

They were quiet as they walked out of the building and climbed into Kayla's cruiser. Jericho made a frustrating call to the rental company as they drove, explaining that his vehicle had been disabled and would need repairs. He asked about getting a replacement, but apparently they weren't impressed with his treatment of the first one and didn't feel like trusting him with a second. He couldn't blame them, but it certainly made things a bit awkward, transportation-wise.

Kayla pulled into the parking lot of the Main Street Diner, the only restaurant in town that served breakfast. At least, it had been the only one back when Jericho had lived there.

"We're going to hang on to your rental for a while," Kayla said as she climbed out of the squad car. "We'll need to collect evidence."

"Any chance of me getting my gear out of it? Just clothes and toiletries. I doubt it'd be evidence of anything but my commitment to personal hygiene."

"I'll see what I can do."

They found a booth toward the back, were served coffees, and then sat staring at each other.

"You're planning on looking into things?" Kayla finally said.

Jericho shrugged. "Probably. If you can give me a good reason to stay out of it, I guess I will, but the feds thinking they can do a better job than someone who knows all the locals? That's not a good reason."

Kayla nodded slowly. "*You* don't know all the locals."

"No. You do. So I thought maybe you'd want to help me out."

"Do you have a plan?"

"Not really. But I have an understanding of the situation, I think."

"Please, share."

Jericho shrugged. "You know the same stuff I do, I think. Whoever took the kids wanted *those* kids. Just Nikki's, not the others in the house. So this wasn't random. Nikki's got no money, so there's no ransom motive." He paused, and Kayla gestured for him to continue. It felt absolutely natural to fall into this rhythm with her: two cops running over the facts of a case before they got into speculation and suspicions. "Whatever Eli was mixed up in, it got him killed, and when that didn't get these people what they wanted, they sent goons to scare it out of Nikki. She says she doesn't know what they want, doesn't *have* what they want, but I'm guessing they think she does, because when the first round didn't work, they upped the ante: burned the house, took the kids. They've got Nikki's attention now, and they're going to try to get what they want from her in exchange for their hostages."

Kayla nodded. "Yeah, that's a fair set of assumptions."

"So we've got two different paths to consider. One is that Nikki doesn't actually have whatever it is these people want and has no way to get whatever it is. If that's the case, we can either try to convince them she doesn't have whatever it is, which is going to be pretty difficult since we don't know who the hell they are or how to get in touch with them, or we can try to work around the whole 'giving them what they want' system and try to find the kids on our own."

"Which is going to be pretty tricky, considering how much space there is up here and how few leads we seem to have."

Jericho nodded. "Yeah. So maybe we should be hoping for the second possibility: that Nikki *does* have what they want, and knows it. In which case the easiest thing is for Nikki to just give whatever it is to whoever it is that wants it. They get what they want, she gets the kids back."

Kayla shook her head. "They've already killed one person over this, if we're assuming that Eli's death was related. Sure, killing a criminal adult is a lot easier than killing two innocent kids, in terms of morality. But there's a risk involved in returning the victims if they heard or saw anything. It'd be safer for our perps to tidy things up completely."

"Yeah, I'm worried about that too," Jericho admitted. "And I'm worried that the feds are so busy building whatever their larger case is that they may not be as focused as they should be on saving Elijah and Nicolette. I'm not saying they won't *try*, but . . ."

Kayla nodded again. She sipped her coffee, then looked up at him, her eyes as clear and forthright as they'd been all those years ago. "So what are we going to do about it?"

"Regardless of what the truth is about Nikki, everything gets better if we find the kids, right? We can get them out of harm's way, and then sort out the rest of it later."

"And you have a plan for how to find them?" she asked with a raised eyebrow.

"A plan? Not quite, no. But hopefully we can get Nikki to talk to us a bit more honestly than she does with the feds. Maybe you'd better stay out of that conversation. Not that she trusts me, either, but she hasn't seen me in a uniform, and we're family, for what that's worth. And I can follow any other leads you give me. Wade said he didn't send the goons—"

"And you believe him?"

Jericho shrugged. "Yeah, I think so. You know Wade. If he doesn't want to answer something, he'll get cagey and avoid the question and play with words or whatever. He doesn't like to lie, not to his friends." He caught himself. "He *didn't* like to lie. Back when we *were* friends."

Kayla was watching him closely. "You've still got a blind spot about him."

"Blind? I don't know. I guess I see him differently, yeah. But I think I do see him. I *did* see him." Maybe he should have moved on, but he'd been trying so hard to *not* think about Wade for too long; now that he had an excuse, he wanted to run with it. "You and him stopped hanging out. Right after I left, or did you stay friends for a while?"

"Jay." She said it like she was surprised, and maybe kind of disappointed. "Wade and I were *never* friends. I mean, the three of us hung out, sure, but it was never about Wade and me. It was you and Wade, and you and me; Wade and I put up with each other for your sake."

That wasn't how Jericho remembered it.

They'd all been children of single parents: Wade's mother had been having too much trouble finding her own way to give any guidance to her son, while Sheriff Morgan and Eli had been too preoccupied with their opposite sides of the criminal life to spend much time with their kids. The sheriff had been more loving than Eli, certainly, more protective and responsible, but he'd had absolutely no idea what to do with his tomboy daughter. And while their parents battled, the children had found peace, at least with each other. Or so Jericho had thought.

"You had enough sense to stay away from the stupid trouble we got into, but . . . You didn't like Wade? I'm sure he liked you."

"He liked knowing he was driving the sheriff crazy, hanging out with his daughter. The same way you liked knowing you were driving the sheriff crazy, *sleeping* with his daughter."

"No," Jericho denied. Then he grinned. "Okay, that was maybe a bit of a bonus, yeah. But it wasn't the main appeal, Kay. I swear."

She gave a gentle snort, but let the argument go. "So if we're assuming that this is all the same people and Wade didn't send the goons, then he also didn't burn the house or take the kids. Right?"

"Right." Jericho hoped it was true; he didn't want to be wrong about something so important, and he also didn't want to think of Wade as the sort of person who would harm children. Or set a house on fire when Jericho was sleeping in it. "So who else is there? Who else was Eli doing business with? If we're lucky, Nikki will know, and she might not tell the feds but maybe she'll tell me. If she even knows; I really have no idea what their relationship was like. Whether Eli would have told her that stuff."

"I'm not sure either. But if she doesn't know, I can still think of some places we could start." She looked like she was considering her next words pretty carefully. "And if you think you can trust Wade Granger—I mean, Jay, you *can't* trust Wade, not on anything important—but if you truly believe he isn't involved and want to trust your instincts on that, he might be able to give you some ideas. And he'd definitely be more likely to share that information with you than with me or anyone else official."

Jericho tried to ignore the twist of excitement in his gut. He was going to see Wade again, but he was going with serious business. This wasn't about Jericho's little crush, it was about solving crimes.

They ordered and ate their breakfasts, Jericho doubling up when he remembered how long it had been since he'd had a proper meal, and then walked back out to the cruiser. "You know anywhere I can rent a car?" he asked.

Kayla shrugged. "Closest real rental place is in Kalispell. But you might want to talk to Scotty Hawk at the garage. He's usually got a few clunkers lying around, and he might not mind making a bit of money off one of them. I can drop you there, if you want. And if you're planning to look for Wade? You can try the bar, but that's pretty public. Kind of an announcement, and you might want to be a bit more subtle. You could ask Scotty how to get hold of him. He and Wade—they spend some time together."

Jericho didn't let his face change, but his mind was racing. Was Kayla saying Wade and this Scotty Hawk were involved? Romantically? What did it mean if they were? And how the hell did Jericho feel about it?

Too many questions and he didn't want to think about any of them. "The garage is in the same place? Lance Wilkins used to run it?" She nodded and he said, "It's not far. I can walk. You going to go back to the station?"

"Yeah. I've got to— I don't know, I've got to make sure I'm supporting the feds however I can. They're still our best bet on all this. They've got the expertise and the resources. Whatever you figure out is just a backup plan. So I'll give you information if I can, and I'll make sure Nikki gets your number when they spring her. And if you need any kind of support, you should let me know. Otherwise, though, I'm following the rules and helping the feds. You understand?"

"Yeah." If Kayla had dropped into his life in LA, it was about the same way he'd have treated her. He'd help as possible, but not to the point that it interfered with his career. And she was right about the feds still being the best bet for solving all of this. He was following up leads they might ignore, but that didn't mean they were *good* leads, really. "Okay. We have a sort-of plan. Keep in touch, and let me know if I can do anything."

"You bet. Thanks for breakfast."

And that was it. Jericho was on his own. He headed down the sidewalk toward the garage, and tried to keep himself from getting worked up about Scotty Hawk and his possible relationship with Wade. It was none of Jericho's business. If Wade had a boyfriend,

Jericho was happy for him. It wasn't like Jericho had been a monk since he left Mosely. Wasn't like he'd thought the whole state of Montana had been dropped into a freezer when he left and he'd come back to find everyone recently thawed and waiting for him with open arms. It wasn't like he even *wanted* Wade; available or not, the man was trouble and Jericho's only smart move was to maintain a professional boundary.

You're walking pretty fast for someone who isn't all that interested in getting somewhere, his inner voice pointed out. It added a completely gratuitous *asshole*, and fell silent.

Jericho made himself slow down. Then he thought about Wade, the warmth of his skin and the strength of his body. And he started walking just a little bit faster.

CHAPTER 8

Scotty Hawk was grossly overweight and about sixty years old. He was wearing greasy sweatpants that clung in all the wrong places, he was chain-smoking Marlboros and he had a serious case of BO. Jericho kind of wanted to hug him. Whatever Kayla had been hinting at, it was pretty damn clear that unless Wade had fallen on *very* hard times, he was not romantically involved with Scotty Hawk.

"Sheriff Morgan said you might have a car I could rent," Jericho said with a bright smile.

Scotty frowned back at him. "The *sheriff* said that, did she?" The derision in his voice made the situation clear. Kayla had said Scotty and Wade spent time together—just like Eli and Wade had spent time together. They were all outlaws, criminals, or at least completely uninterested in respecting authority. Wade and Scotty had a *professional* relationship.

"She did. And she said you might be able to help me get in contact with Wade Granger."

Dropping that name earned Jericho a slightly less derisive expression. "Wade *know* you're looking for him?"

"I doubt it. Probably if he knew, he'd give me a call. I'm not asking for any secrets, but if you could get a message to him for me, that'd be great."

"You're Eli Crewe's boy?" Scotty looked thoughtful and added a grudging, "Sorry for your loss." He dropped the butt of his cigarette and crushed it under his boot. "You poking into all that? Trying to figure out what happened to him?"

Jericho didn't want to paint such a clear target on himself. "No. I'm just here for the funeral, I guess. And to help Nikki sort things out."

Scotty snorted. "Have fun with that." He gave Jericho another once-over, then said, "Yeah, I've got a car you can rent. Fifty bucks a day. You give me your credit card information before you leave the place."

"Fifty bucks? That's pretty steep."

"Take it or leave it."

Apparently Jericho's family connections were only going to take him so far. "Fine. I'll take it. And can you get a message to Wade for me? Or tell me where I might find him?"

"The lady cop didn't give you that information?"

"Nope."

Another long look. Jericho was beginning to wish he'd shaved that morning, or at least brushed his teeth. But possibly appearing *more* respectable wouldn't have the desired effect on someone like Scotty. "I'll let him know you're looking for him," Scotty finally said. "You can leave your phone number with me."

Jericho left the information and let himself be led around the back of the garage. Scotty gestured to a baby-blue pickup truck, old enough for the frame to be squared off instead of having the rounded, bulging lines of the modern versions.

"Does it run?" Jericho asked.

Scotty drew back as if insulted. "I'm a *mechanic*." He gave the truck a rough thump on the hood and shrugged. "I don't do body work. But the engine is solid."

So Jericho climbed in, adjusted the vinyl bench seat as far back as it would go, and cranked the window down to get a little fresh air into the musty cab. There was a crack in the windshield, a gaping hole where the radio should be . . . and when he turned the key, the ignition caught right away and the engine purred like a kitten. Okay. He could work with this.

Kayla called as he was pulling out of the garage, and said he could pick up his gear from the rental at the sheriff's station. He had a vehicle, he would soon have his stuff; things were starting to come together. But when he was almost to the station he saw a woman stomping along the sidewalk and realized it was Nikki. She was out of the sheriff's office, and she hadn't called him. He should have known things were going too smoothly.

He pulled over in front of her and climbed out of the truck. She stared at him as if she was startled, almost afraid, and he found himself speaking to her in low, soothing tones. "Hey, Nikki. It's me. New truck, sorry. They let you go? Do you need a ride somewhere?"

She looked feral, her eyes darting wildly, as if she was about to run away. Or attack. "Leave me alone!"

"What? I talked to Kayla—Sheriff Morgan—and I think she's on our side. You know, she needs to follow the rules, but—"

"No! Leave it alone! The police are taking care of it. The FBI. They've got it under control and they don't need any help. You'll just get in the way." She was shaking, and grabbed hold of the sides of her sweatpants as if hoping they'd keep her hands still. "Go home," she almost yelled. "Nobody wants you here."

"I don't get it. What changed?"

"Nothing! But the cops told me what to do. They said I have to be cool and not push on this. I don't want some fucking urban cowboy charging in and messing things up! You don't want to be here, so this should be good news for you. Go home!"

He didn't know her well enough to know if this sort of one-eighty was typical. "You're satisfied with what they're doing to get the kids back?" he asked carefully.

"Obviously. Yes. Now fuck off. I don't need your help."

It was tempting to take advantage of the offer. Everything would be a hell of a lot cleaner if he got out of Mosely, and got the hell away from this crazy woman, as soon as he could. But his conscience would crucify him if he left without being sure he'd done all he could to help. Nikki's husband had died two days ago, her children had just been kidnapped—it wasn't too surprising that she was missing some of the finer points of etiquette. And the kids themselves? Damn it, the kids needed him, whether Nikki liked it or not.

"Where are you staying? Do you have friends you want to call? I mean, okay, if you want me to stay out of the investigation, I can do that. But that doesn't mean I can't help at all. I was going to get a room at the motel. You want me to get one for you too?"

"I want you to *fuck off*," she growled, but he could tell she was weakening. Her hands were shaking again, her grip on her pants sending tremors up and down the fabric on her legs, and he'd seen her expression on too many faces before, faces of people who'd been pushed beyond their breaking point and were just trying to hold themselves together long enough to be able to fall apart in safety.

"Come sit in the truck, at least," he said softly. "I rented it from Scotty Hawk at the garage. It looks like shit, but the engine's good so far. I can take you where you're going."

She seemed like she might keep fighting, but finally her head flopped down as if the muscles of her neck had been snapped, and she stumbled over to the passenger side of the truck.

He moved quickly and got them on the road before she changed her mind. "Motel?" he asked quietly.

She didn't respond, so he decided to assume she agreed.

He was nervous about leaving her alone in the truck when he went in to book rooms, but he figured she'd be better in the quiet than in the motel office. He filled out the forms, collected the keys, and went out to pull her door open. "Come on. You should have a shower, maybe. Sleep a bit. If you tell me your size and what you need, I can try to pick up a couple changes of clothes. Bathroom stuff. Whatever."

She scowled at him. "Why are you being so nice?"

"I have no idea."

"This is just what you're like? Eli said—"

"I don't think I need to hear any more of Eli's opinions, thanks."

"He said you were soft," she said as if he hadn't interrupted.

"Compared to him? I absolutely am. Now, come on. You can get settled in."

She followed him, and he tried to guess how long he could count on this new obedience lasting. Probably not long, so he'd better enjoy it while he could.

The whole situation felt too mundane. He should be doing something about the kids, not babysitting their damaged mother. But maybe she was right. Not about him being a cowboy, but maybe about staying out of things when he didn't know the full picture. A kidnapping was always a tense situation, and it would be a lot easier to forgive himself for doing nothing, even if it ended badly for the kids, than for doing the wrong thing and being actively responsible for whatever happened to them. *I wonder if Eli told her you're a coward,* his inner voice mused.

Having common sense isn't being cowardly, he retorted to the annoying voice. He made sure Nikki was as settled as possible and told her he'd be back in a bit, then walked the few blocks to Finnigan's. Bigger than a general store, he supposed it was a department store, technically, but too small to really deserve the name. But it was where he'd find women's clothes. He bought everything in size large, hoping it was about right. Nikki was tall and heavy-boned, but she wasn't fat. And everything he picked up felt stretchy, so hopefully size wouldn't matter too much. The woman at the cash register gave him a curious look, as if she wasn't used to customers she didn't recognize, but he didn't explain himself and she didn't press.

He was walking back to the motel when his phone rang, an unfamiliar number on the caller ID. "Hello?"

"I heard you were asking after me." Wade's voice was smooth and easy and warmed Jericho's gut like a sip of fine whiskey.

"Uh, yeah. But maybe not anymore." Well, that wasn't quite true. But Jericho didn't have an *excuse* anymore.

"We should talk," Wade said. He didn't offer any further explanation.

Jericho didn't think he could make himself argue. "Okay. Where and when?"

A pickup only a few years newer than Jericho's rental pulled up beside him, and he glanced over to see Wade in the driver's seat.

"Here and now?" Wade suggested, his voice clear in Jericho's ear as his lips moved behind the closed truck window. "Get in. We'll go for a drive."

Jericho didn't let himself think about all the different reasons he should stay the hell out of Wade Granger's pickup. He just tossed the shopping bags in the back of the truck, then opened the passenger door and slid inside.

Wade drove like he did everything else: confident and relaxed and easy, but with a sharp edge underneath it all, a suggestion that he was ready to go as fast and hard as might be necessary. He didn't seem to be in any hurry to get anywhere or to say anything right then, though, so Jericho tried to sit back and enjoy the ride. But as Wade pulled out onto the highway, Jericho said, "I'm helping Nikki. Looking after her, kind of. I shouldn't be away from the motel for too long."

"You sure got tame, Jay."

"I grew up. Taking responsibility for other people is a pain in the ass, but the world would be a pretty ugly place if we didn't do it."

"And Nikki's worth taking responsibility for?"

"She's my father's widow, so she's family. And she doesn't seem to have anyone else."

"Interesting how you start caring about family now, when you didn't for the last fifteen years."

"Is this what you thought we needed to talk about?"

Wade didn't answer right away, and when he finally did, he sounded almost regretful. "No, not completely. A little bit, though."

"Oh, okay. That's clear."

Wade pulled off the highway into a small gravel area with room enough for a few cars to park. There was a pathway leading into the forest with a metal sign posted beside it. "You do any hiking out there in LA?"

"Not much."

"Well, we won't go too far, then. After all, you've got to get back to Nikki."

The inner voice said, *You're the one who wanted to spend time with him, asshole.*

So Jericho climbed out of the truck and followed Wade toward the path. Wade's black jeans and work boots appeared the same as the day before; his gray dress shirt was damn similar too, but judging by the sharp crease on its sleeve, it was fresh that morning. He seemed pretty fresh in general, really, and Jericho wished he'd had time to pick up his gear and shave.

"So what *do* you do with your time out there in the big city?" Wade asked over his shoulder. When the path widened, he stepped to one side and waited for Jericho to come up beside him.

"I work."

"What *else* do you do?" Wade smiled like a doting uncle encouraging a reluctant nephew to share details of his day at school. "What do you do for fun? Who do you hang out with?"

"I work for fun, and I hang out with cops. What did you want to talk about, Wade?"

"You don't hang out with cops," Wade said. Not confrontational, just corrective. "I can see you doing the job; you always did like helping people, and you're brave enough to not worry about the risks. And sure, maybe you work a lot of hours. But you don't hang out with cops when you're not on the clock." There was no hint of a question in the words. As if Wade figured he knew Jericho well enough to know who his friends were. The worst part was that Wade was right.

"No, I guess I don't."

"So you play sports? Go out to clubs or some other city shit? What are you missing because you're stuck up here babysitting your stepmother?"

"I run. Go to the gym. Play some basketball. Clubs and city shit now and then. What about you? Besides your busy life of bar ownership and petty crime, I mean."

Wade grinned at him. "Oh, there's not room for too much besides all that. Petty crime isn't just a career, it's a *lifestyle*."

It certainly had been for Eli. Jericho might like to think that Wade was doing better than Eli had, but there was no reason to believe it was true. "I thought you were dating Scotty Hawk."

Wade stopped and turned to stare at him. "What?"

"Kayla said something, and I guess I misinterpreted it." Jericho felt foolish, but somehow it was okay to feel that way around Wade, even after so long. He kept walking, though, because it was nice to not have to look at Wade during his confession. Wade jogged to catch up, and Jericho added, "In my defense, I hadn't met him yet. Once I saw him, I . . . reassessed."

"Jay, be careful now. I don't want to hear you say anything disrespectful about my boyfriend."

Jericho glanced over and saw Wade's wide, genuine smile, and he had a similar expression on his own face. It was good. Great, even. The two of them, together, joking and laughing. It was like they were on the same team, like it always had when they were younger. Jericho knew, he *knew*, that if he moved toward Wade, he'd be met with open arms, a bear hug that would wrap him in the warmth and simple affection he'd been missing for far too long. But he had no idea what would happen when the hug was over, so he made himself keep moving.

"I'm single," Wade said into the void. "I have . . . friends, I guess. Nothing special."

If Jericho responded with his own status, it would make this conversation something different. Something he wasn't quite ready to deal with. *Eli always said you were a chickenshit*, his inner voice taunted.

"Your mom still around?" Possibly a painful subject, given Wade's relationship with his mother, but maybe that was all old news. The two of them could have reconciled and be best buddies by now. After all, Jericho had been away a long time.

But Wade made a familiar grimace and said, "She's still in town. Out of the business, thank god. Not doing too much of anything anymore."

It *was* a relief to know she was out of the business. There was nothing good about being a fiftysomething prostitute in small-town Montana. Or anywhere else, but somehow being in a small town made the idea seem just a little bit worse. "You never left? Never had the urge to get the hell out of here and make a fresh start somewhere else? Try a new life?"

Wade shook his head. His smile now was a little more sad, but no less genuine. "There's some people who are only suited for one thing, Jay."

"That may be true. But I don't think you're one of them. At least, you didn't used to be."

They walked in silence for a while. The light coming through the trees was dappled green, and the pine needles underfoot cushioned each step, making it feel like they were walking on a quilt.

They reached a small clearing with a fallen tree on one side, and Wade lowered himself gracefully onto the trunk, then looked up at Jericho. "You got Nikki figured out yet?"

Jericho snorted. "Not even close."

Wade nodded. "Took me a while too." He leaned back and stretched his legs out, his face tilted to catch whatever sunlight penetrated the thick trees. "I used to think it was weird, her and Eli hooking up. Then I got to know her."

"And that made it make sense?"

"They're two of a kind, Jay. Maybe Nikki hides it a bit better, especially with people like you—those predisposed to *chivalry*." His smile was wolfish, making it clear he considered this predisposition to be one of Jericho's weaknesses.

"She loves her kids. She just about fell apart when she heard they were missing."

"You saying Eli didn't love you?"

Jericho frowned. "I don't think I need to *say* it. You were there."

"He wasn't Ward Cleaver, I'll give you that. But remember how he took on Terry Maine when Terry was giving you a hard time about that car you sold him?"

"Eli hated Terry from when they were in high school. He would have been happy for any excuse to fight with him."

Wade shrugged. "He was fighting for his kid."

"His *pride*, maybe. It's easy to pretend you're acting out of love when you're doing what you want to do anyway. If Eli had ever *not* fought someone, *that* might have been a sign he cared."

"You always did have high standards."

Jericho turned and looked into the forest. Enough history. There was no point worrying about it anymore. "You're saying Nikki's like Eli—does that mean she was part of his business ventures?"

"She might have helped out some. But she was never completely his partner. Not because she wasn't interested or willing, just because most of the men Eli dealt with were pretty old school. They thought the womenfolk should stay at home cooking and cleaning. Wasn't worth the fight to get them to accept her."

"Weren't *you* one of the men Eli dealt with?"

"I'm the modern version."

"Kinder and gentler?"

"I don't know about that. But less sexist, at least. Less racist."

"Baby steps."

"That's right." Wade tilted his gaze in Jericho's direction, squinting against the sunlight. "You know what Nikki was doing yesterday afternoon? Where she was driving your truck?"

"She said she had errands." But she hadn't even bought groceries. "I guess you could call it that."

"Any chance you could just *tell* me what she was doing?"

But Wade didn't seem interested in being rushed. "What do you think the biggest challenge is, for someone in my line of work?"

"Picking out which gray shirt to wear each day?"

"That *is* tricky. But even harder than that?"

Jericho didn't need to think too much. "Staying out of jail, I'd imagine."

"Bingo." Wade's smile felt like an only slightly ironic congratulations. "We worry about local cops, sure. The sheriff's department is an annoyance, especially since Kayla took over—she's *tenacious*. But what worries us most is the feds. Sniffing around, trying to put things together. They're a big problem."

"I'm really sorry to hear that."

Wade smiled. "If someone had something that would make the feds go away—make them leave us alone, at least—that'd be valuable."

It was Jericho's turn to squint. "Valuable enough to kill for? To kidnap kids for?" He paused. "And what the hell would you have that would make the feds go away?"

"Me? I don't have anything. *Nikki*, though? Nikki might have something pretty damn good. And she spent yesterday afternoon driving around town, offering it for sale to the highest bidder."

CHAPTER 9

Jericho's head was beginning to ache. "Offering *what* for sale?"

"Evidence. She showed me a video clip—I guess there's probably stuff you'd need to do to authenticate it or whatever, but if it's real . . ." He blew a low whistle. "It showed three feds—guys I recognized—taking money from Casey Donovan. He was the president of the Mountaineers for about twenty years. They do a lot of cross-border stuff, so definitely federal jurisdiction. And this clip made it look like he was *close* with these three feds."

"It could be undercover work. Authorized as part of a larger operation."

"Could be." Wade didn't look convinced. "But you know why he's not the president of the club anymore, Jay? He's dead. Washed up in the lake last fall with six bullets in his brain. Unsolved murder." Wade was watching Jericho closely now. "Know what happened after he died? Some goons tore his house apart, searching for something. Donovan's crew are bikers, so they buddied up and fought back. But somehow things calmed down there. Turned out maybe the bikers didn't have whatever it was the goons were looking for."

"You think they were looking for the video?"

"Seems likely."

"I don't see the connection, though. How would Nikki have gotten hold of it?"

Wade sighed. "Eli and Donovan did time together, down at Deer Lodge a few years ago. They did some business afterward. I was maybe involved in a few deals with them." He frowned. "I don't think they were so close that Donovan would really *trust* Eli, but if he was desperate enough—or if Eli saw something lying around and thought he could make use of it, he might have lifted it. I don't know the details, but Nikki's got the video, so I guess that's what happened."

Jericho's head was spinning. "Three feds. Which ones?"

"I don't have their names. I've just seen them hanging out with the others."

"You think— Let me run through it, okay? You think somehow the bikers recorded their business with the feds. The feds found out about the video—maybe the bikers tried to blackmail them with it? The feds tried to get it back from the bikers, and Casey Donovan ended up dead as a result."

Jericho paused to see if Wade had anything to add, but he just nodded his agreement, so Jericho continued. "Donovan hid or gave away the recording before the feds showed up, or else Eli stole it. Eli sat on it for a while and then tried to use it. Probably blackmail, either for cash or for them turning a blind eye to his activities. The feds didn't want to play along, so they killed him." It was one thing for a fellow criminal to have killed Eli, but a fed? Fuck, no. That was not allowed.

Wade took over. "But he didn't have what they were looking for on his body, so they went to the house. Threatening Nikki didn't work, so they burned the house down and took the kids. Now they're holding the kids and they're going to try to trade them for the video."

Jericho nodded slowly as another piece fit into the puzzle. "Shit."

"What?"

"Nikki turned on me after spending time with the FBI. I don't know which agents—I've only met one of the FBI guys—" He stopped. No. Hell no. "He was asking more questions about Nikki than about Eli. I thought it was just because he believed me when I said that I'd had no contact for years, but . . . I told him Nikki might have whatever the goons were looking for; I told him she'd do whatever was best for her fucking *kids*." Jericho's stomach tightened. It was a jump, one Jericho really, really didn't want to make, but it fit the rest of the situation. "I thought maybe the kidnappers had gotten a message to her and warned her not to make waves, but I couldn't see how they'd have reached her when she was stuck in a damn interrogation room without a cell phone."

"Not too hard to reach her if the kidnappers are the ones interrogating her."

"Yeah. But would she be that stupid in the first place, trying to sell the video? Two men dead, and she charged in anyway?"

"Well, she's stubborn. Desperate, too, probably: two kids to support and she's not likely to get a job with her criminal record."

"She's got a record?"

"That's my understanding, but I admit, I don't know details. I figured you'd have a line on that."

"I didn't know she existed until I was far away from any of my record-checking tools." Jericho sank down onto the log beside Wade, careful to keep a safe distance between them. "She didn't tell me Eli was dead when she called me. She wanted me to come out so she'd have some protection while she was doing all this."

"Off-duty cop in the house? Not bad. Not just for the muscle, but for the legitimacy. If she ended up dead, it'd be easy for the feds to cover that up, but it'd be harder to cover up something happening to a respectable citizen like you. And she didn't go to the feds with the video, as far as I know. She wasn't quite *that* crazy. I think she was just shopping it around to locals who might find it useful. So maybe she hoped the feds would never think she had it."

"Then how would they have known what she was doing?"

"They've got rats in at least one of the operations in town."

"*Operations*? Like, multiple criminal organizations? In a place this small?"

Wade snorted. "Since the mine shut down, I think the biggest industry up here is smuggling shit across the border in one direction or the other. If you plan it right, you can take something with you *and* bring something back. Guns up and pot back is the standard pattern, but I've seen a lot of other stuff moving too. And once you've got merchandise on this side, there has to be packaging, storage, distribution . . . and support services for the people who do all that work. It's the only thing that's keeping this town alive, and the local cops know it. They don't push us too hard as long as we keep things tidy. Well, the old sheriff didn't. Kay's pushier, and the feds are another matter entirely."

"So why didn't you buy the video? You had a way to get the feds off your back for good, and you didn't take it?"

"I had a way to get *three* feds off my back. And that'd probably be enough, for as long as they were stationed here. They could have leaked me the information I'd need to keep me safe, planted some stuff to throw the other feds off my trail—it would have been convenient. But they'd get transferred eventually, and in the meantime I'd have gotten sloppy. Careless. Nikki was asking far too much for something that wouldn't do me all *that* much good."

"So you said no, she went to someone else—and somehow the feds found out."

"Looks that way. I mean, maybe not. Nikki said there was other stuff on the drive. More clips. She wouldn't show me unless I paid, but maybe she showed someone else. Or maybe one of the other organizations in town found out about the feds video and decided they wanted it without paying for it. So they knocked off Eli, tried to scare Nikki, and then upped their game by taking the kids."

"Maybe. But you're right, the evidence wouldn't be *that* valuable to any of the locals. Useful, but maybe not important enough to go this far. The local criminals wouldn't have as much to gain as the feds would have to lose. They're the ones with the highest stakes in all this. And they're the ones Nikki was talking to when she decided I needed to stop asking questions." Jericho hoped he was wrong, but there was definitely enough to look at. "Most of the feds aren't dirty. I can contact someone in DC and get them looking at it."

"Risky. If they come charging in, our boys could spook and hurt the kids."

"The people I'd contact are professionals. They'd know enough to be subtle."

"You've got no proof on any of this. You believe me because . . . well, because you've always been a bit of a sucker that way. But the feds won't, even if I was stupid enough to talk to them, which I'm not. And nobody else will be stupid enough either." Wade was watching Jericho closely, now. His voice was softer, more persuasive as he said, "If the feds believed you one hundred percent, that'd be great. We could back off and let them take over. If they believed you zero percent, that'd be fine too: they'd write you off as a crackpot, and there'd be no harm done. But they're going to believe you somewhere in the middle, right? Enough to look into things, but not enough to take it totally seriously. *That's* where the trouble's going to come from."

Jericho wished he could disagree, but Wade had a point. "So what do you suggest? How do you think we should be handling it?"

"We should look into it. See what we can come up with. If we can get some hard evidence, something the feds would believe, then great—we go with them. If we can't, we find the kids ourselves. We *handle it* ourselves."

"Fucking cowboy bullshit."

"You always swear when you're thinking."

"No." Jericho shook his head impatiently "You don't know that. Not anymore. You don't know *me* anymore. But here's a quick reminder, Wade: I'm a cop, not a vigilante."

"You're a cop because you care about the law? Or because you want to do the right thing?" Wade's tone made it clear which option he thought was accurate.

But for once, Jericho could shove Wade's know-it-all garbage back down his throat. "*Both*," he growled. There were parts of his job he didn't like—the tedium, the futility—but he was good with the general principles. "The right thing *is* the law. People living together in groups? They need rules. They need consistency, and they need to know there's someone there to enforce things when someone breaks the rules. Following the law *is* doing the right thing."

Wade shook his head, his frown a little overdone. "Still with that black-and-white thinking, huh?" He rose to his feet, an abrupt but still somehow graceful movement. "Okay. Do it your way. I mean, they're your family. I shouldn't even be involved—I was just being nostalgic, I guess. No room for that, though; you're a *lawman* now. You've got to follow the rules, no matter what."

Jericho stood up as well. "It's that simple for you? And if we screw it up and something happens to the kids—something that might *not* have happened if we'd gone to the feds and told them what we knew—you can just walk away from that. You don't let shit like that bother you, right? You've probably got some bullshit rationale already worked up. 'Everybody dies sooner or later.' Is that the one you're going to use? Or maybe 'Hey, at least we tried.' That's a good all-purpose get-out-of-guilt-free card. Or 'The universe is unknowable and uncontrollable, but it takes courage to accept that.'"

He watched as those words hit home. Wade looked surprised, as if he'd thought maybe Jericho would have forgotten them. Which was pretty good proof that Wade really *didn't* know Jericho anymore. All those years ago, when Jericho had been talking about getting the hell out of Mosely and taking control of his life, Wade had laughed at him and said it was impossible. He'd said no one was actually driving the cars they were riding in, and if Jericho would just stop trying to steer, he might be able to enjoy the ride a little more. Wade had refused to leave town, and finally, Jericho had refused to stay. But he'd never forgotten Wade's arguments, and he probably never would.

"You think running to the feds is taking control of things?" Wade asked. "No. It's just your way of protecting yourself. Because you know I'm right, that it *is* all uncontrollable, and you want to make sure there's someone else to blame."

"So if it's uncontrollable, there's no reason for anyone to do anything. We should all just get high and fuck around and do whatever feels good in any given moment. That's what you think? There's sure no reason for us to risk our necks poking around in an investigation, or to do any other goddamn thing with our lives."

Wade looked at the forest floor for a moment or two, then up at Jericho. "I really missed you, Jay. Nobody else yells at me like you do."

Nobody else got Jericho frustrated enough that he *wanted* to yell, but he wasn't going to tell Wade that. It would be one more response that would move them into dangerous territory, too intimate and true for who they now were.

"We should get back," he said. "We don't have evidence *yet*, but if I can get that video clip from Nikki, we're home free. I can send it to my captain in LA, and she'll know the best feds to forward it to. They'll take care of all of it." And Jericho would return to LA where he belonged.

"I yield to your wisdom and experience." Wade's tone made it clear he was doing no such thing but wasn't going to fight about it anymore.

Jericho let it go, and they drove back to the motel in silence. As Wade pulled into the parking lot, Jericho said, "Thanks for the heads-up. The background. Everything makes a lot more sense, now. I don't really *like* it, but I can understand it."

"Unless I'm lying about all of it for my own dark purposes," Wade said. He didn't look over at Jericho.

"No," Jericho said. "Lying about some of it? Sure, maybe. Dark purposes? I wouldn't be surprised. But you wouldn't make the whole story up."

"So now is it my turn to say you don't know me anymore?"

"You can if you want to. But it won't do you any good. I'll still know what I know."

"And I'll still know that you swear when you're thinking," Wade said calmly as Jericho pushed the truck door open. "Some things don't change, Jay."

Jericho glanced over and found his gaze caught by Wade's deep-gray eyes. *"Some things don't change."* They knew each other, just like they always had. And as they stared across the worn bench seat of the pickup, the air crackled between them, and they *wanted* each other, just like they always had.

Jericho slid out of the truck so fast he almost fell over when his feet hit the sidewalk. He pulled himself together enough to grab his shopping bags from the back, then turned to the motel. And stared at the empty spot where his rental pickup should have been.

He strode across the parking lot and banged on the door of the room he'd rented for Nikki. No answer. Lucky that he'd had the foresight to ask for two keys. He banged again, then fumbled in his pocket for the key. The door swung open to show an empty room, the bed unrumpled by so much as a nap.

"Son of a bitch." Jericho crossed the room in four strides and looked into the bathroom, but he'd known it would be empty.

Nikki was gone, and she'd taken his truck.

CHAPTER 10

"Well, you *wanted* to stay out of it." Wade's voice came from the doorway. His tone was light, but he was watching Jericho closely as he stepped inside, clearly waiting for something.

Waiting for what, though? How the hell was Jericho supposed to react to this? He ran his hands through his hair and thought longingly of the simplicity of Los Angeles. "How the hell did she get the truck started? I've got the key."

"That criminal record I mentioned?" Wade said. "Grand theft auto, as I understand it. Maybe some other stuff too, but she wouldn't have to be an expert to hotwire an old truck. Hell, Scotty likely had the wires already stripped."

Jericho wanted to kick something, or possibly someone. "You think she's gone to meet them?"

"Maybe she just got tired of waiting for you and went to do her own shopping. But, yeah, I think she went to meet them."

Jericho's mind raced. "They can't let her walk away. Even if she gives them the original, they can't be sure she didn't make copies. If they give her the kids and let her leave, they'll be back where they started, with a bonus kidnapping charge to worry about."

"She might have a plan. She could tell them she set up a dead man's switch . . . Hell, maybe she did."

"Could be electronic," Jericho mused. "Like an email that gets sent if she doesn't log onto a certain account regularly." He cut his gaze toward Wade. "I didn't see a computer at the house. Would she know how to do that?"

"Probably not," Wade admitted. "Eli had an old laptop—she might have it stashed away somewhere, if it's still working. But I don't think they ever did much on the internet. Not even email."

"She could have given a copy to someone. Not a lawyer, not with the way she hates authority. A friend? She must have *some* friends or family somewhere, right?"

"Not that I ever heard of." Wade shrugged. "Of course, me not knowing about the person would be *good*, if she actually did set something up. If no one's ever heard of them, nobody's going to be able to find them."

"She didn't mention anybody, though." Jericho wasn't sure how much he should trust a word Nikki had said, but he couldn't see a reason for her to have lied, at least in that one limited area. "When we were looking for somewhere safe to stash the kids last night, she ended up sending them to the snotty neighbors. She wouldn't have done that if she had anyone else to ask."

"Maybe just no one close. But she could email the video anywhere she wanted if she found a computer."

"Yeah. Fuck." If he'd been back in LA, there would have been things he could do: he could search for Nikki's criminal record and known associates, check a number of databases to see if he could figure out where she'd been and who she'd been connected to. He could get the tech guys trying to trace her internet traffic, assuming there'd been any. But here, operating as a civilian? He didn't have any of those resources. Maybe he could phone a friend on the force back in the city and get them to check for him.

Except Wade had been right when he'd said Jericho didn't hang out with cops. He didn't have friends on the force, not really. He'd had partners, sure, but none that he'd bonded with, not like the cops on the TV shows did. Not like some of the other cops he'd seen in real life did. If there was an official inquiry to be made, Jericho had lots of people he could contact who respected him as a professional. But something unofficial? Off the books?

"We should call Kayla," he said.

Wade stared at him for a moment, then returned in the same measured tone, "Or maybe we should cut our thumbs off."

"No, it makes sense. Even if it's just a question of letting her know—I mean, Wade, we have to let her know there's crooked feds working out of her department! She needs to be aware of that for her own safety. And she could help us on this. She could run checks on Nikki, get us good information."

"Kayla's a *cop*, Jay!"

"Jesus, Wade, so am I. Are you forgetting that somehow?"

"I'm trying to, yeah! It's a bit easier since you do your cop thing so far away. But Kayla's in my face every fucking day. She's—"

"Doing her job? Serving and protecting the citizens of Mosely County?"

"*I'm* a citizen of Mosely County."

"Well, if you've been dissatisfied with her service, I'm sure she'd like to hear from you. But in the meantime, there are two kidnapped children and a pain-in-the-ass adult to worry about, so it's too fucking bad if you've got a fucking grudge against Kayla! If she can help, she's in."

"Remember when I said I missed you yelling at me?"

"You said it about a half hour ago, Wade. I remember."

"I was wrong. *You're* the pain in the ass, not Nikki."

"I think it's possible for two people to be ass pains at the same time. You don't have to pick just one of us."

"Good. You're *both* pains in the ass."

"We should call Kayla."

Wade stared at him. "When did this become 'we'?" he asked. It sounded like he was talking to himself as much as to Jericho. "What the hell am I getting involved for?"

"Because there are innocent kids at risk." And then, even though he knew it was stupid and dangerous and opening doors that were better left closed, he added, "Because I need your help." At least he managed to keep himself from adding *because it's always been "we."*

Wade looked like he'd heard the words Jericho hadn't said. They were both quiet for a moment, then Wade crossed to the door and peered at the parking lot. "So call her," he said.

"We used to all be friends," Jericho said as he pulled out his phone.

"No," Wade corrected. "You and me used to be friends. And you and her used to be friends. Me and her? We—we put up with each other."

Strange to hear Kayla's version of the situation confirmed so tidily, and stranger still to realize Jericho had spent years hanging out with both of them, thinking they were all close. He really had been a clueless kid, but he supposed it didn't matter right then.

"You can put up with each other a little longer," he tried. "I'm sure shit's gone down since I left, considering your jobs, but this is too important. You guys can get past it."

Wade didn't object with more than a scowl, so Jericho dialed, and when Kayla answered he said, "Breakfast was so delicious I think we should have lunch too. Maybe out at the cave? I can bring sandwiches."

"The cave?" Kayla sounded uncertain, and he willed her to understand. "Okay," she said slowly. "I'll see you there in . . . half an hour?"

"Great," Jericho said. "See you there."

He hung up and headed for the doorway, Wade falling in behind him as they left the motel.

They didn't talk much as they crossed the street to the grocery store and ordered sandwiches from the little deli in the back. Jericho wasn't actually hungry, and it felt stupid to be taking time for snacks, but they'd have to wait for Kayla anyway, and it was good to keep himself occupied.

The store had the same warped hardwood floors, narrow aisles, and dim lighting he remembered. No need to renovate when it was the only option in town, and any tourists who stumbled in probably appreciated the rustic charm. It had been the only grocery experience Jericho had known for the first half of his life, and he could still remember the shock of walking into a modern supermarket in the city, with all the lights and space and shining food.

From the old grocery store, they walked down the street to the high school, through the parking lot and up the steep path leading into the tree line.

"I haven't been up here in years," Wade said from close behind Jericho.

"Well, that's sad. I thought you'd have preserved it as a shrine to our misspent youth."

"If I turned every place we ever got in trouble into a shrine, the whole damn town would be holy."

"Except the church."

"Kinda hard to get in trouble somewhere we never spent any time."

The path gradually narrowed and became more overgrown, and Jericho had to stop walking and try to get his bearings. "Nobody goes to the cave anymore?"

Wade seemed just as nonplussed. "Too busy playing video games and messing around on their phones?"

Jericho didn't have a better explanation.

"Through here, I think," Wade said. "Kayla'll be coming from the other side, right? She'll park at the end of Division Street?"

"I don't know. Probably. That was my thinking, at least."

"You don't want her seen with us."

"Not by the kidnappers, no."

They pushed through the undergrowth, stumbled around for a while, and finally found the rocky outcrop with its once-familiar handholds. "After you," Wade said, eying Jericho and the cliff face doubtfully.

"You going to catch me if I fall?"

"I'm going to get the hell out of the way. You've put on some weight since the last time I saw you."

"You'd better not be calling me fat, Granger." Jericho started climbing. It *was* a bit trickier than it had been when he was a whip-thin seventeen-year-old, but his added bulk was all muscle, so he had more than enough power to pull himself up the rock. When he hit the top, he slung a leg over onto the flat ledge, then rolled the rest of the way. He peered into the shallow cave in the cliff behind him to make sure it was empty, then stayed on his stomach and looked over the edge of the tiny plateau to see Wade climbing slow and easy. Jericho tossed a pebble down and watched it bounce off Wade's dark head. He found another, slightly larger one and let it go.

Wade's head jerked, and he lifted his face to stare at Jericho. "Throw another one," he growled. "I fucking dare you."

Well, if it was a dare . . . Wade was close enough now that the rock wouldn't pick up much speed, so Jericho found one the size of a walnut and let it fall.

"Son of a bitch," Wade roared, and he surged up what was left of the cliff, aggressive and laughing and perfect.

Jericho rolled away, then scrambled backward, but Wade had always been quicker than him. It was like a panther attacking a tiger, except the tiger was laughing too hard to really fight back.

"I couldn't help myself," Jericho tried.

"Neither can I." Wade grabbed a handful of whatever he could find on the surface of the ledge and drove himself forward, the dirt heading for Jericho's mouth.

They wrestled, testing each other's new bodies, new strengths. Jericho should be paying attention to more serious things. His father was dead, the kids and Nikki were in trouble. Jericho should be fixing his broken world. Instead he was laughing, sparring, letting Wade pin him, but never letting the handful of dirt get too close to his face. The strange, almost frightening familiarity of the contact took Jericho back in time, back to before life got so complicated. Back to when it had just been him and Wade, both knowing the other's body just as well as his own.

Eventually Jericho was flat on his back, Wade straddling him, Jericho's hand locked on Wade's wrist. They were balanced for a moment, Wade's better angle against Jericho's strength, locked in a stalemate. And then Wade's free hand moved. Slowly. Leaving lots of time for Jericho to object, but he stayed still as Wade eased his weight away and let Jericho relax his arm.

Wade's eyes were wide and deep gray and Jericho couldn't stop staring into them. Wade ran his free hand up over Jericho's ribs, barely touching, then over his shoulder and onto the bare skin of his neck. It felt like he was exploring, learning the new dimensions of a body he'd once known as well as he knew his own. He stretched his thumb up Jericho's chin, along his jawline, and then back down his cheek toward his lips. Jericho shivered at the touch like it was making his skin come alive, turning him from stone back into living, *needing* flesh. "Can't help myself," Wade whispered.

Jericho didn't trust his voice, so he just nodded. Wade twisted his wrist in Jericho's grip, and Jericho released him, freeing that hand for whatever Wade wanted to do with it. The dirt Wade had been holding rained down onto the ledge, and Jericho found his own hand coming to rest on the outside of Wade's thigh.

And then there was the gentle scuffing sound of someone climbing the cliff. Wade didn't move, just perched there and waited to see how Jericho would react. Just like it had always been, Wade taking dares, pushing them both to the brink of discovery, and making Jericho protect them.

"Move," Jericho hissed, and there it was, the same disappointment Wade always showed when Jericho wouldn't be quite as crazy as he wanted him to be.

"Make me," Wade challenged.

Jericho heaved. Wade might be quicker, but Jericho had been bigger and stronger even when they were kids. It wasn't hard to dislodge Wade, and once Jericho was free, he didn't let himself think, just leaned over and saw Kayla climbing the rock face toward them.

He didn't say anything until her face appeared, and she only glanced at Jericho before staring at Wade. "Yeah," she said glumly. "That's what I was afraid of."

"He's got good information," Jericho said. "Stuff you need to hear."

"Is it going to help me understand why Nikki Crewe took your truck from the motel and drove out to the middle of nowhere?"

"You had someone tailing her? Wait, just you, or the feds? Who knows where she is? And is anyone with her now? Any of *your* people?"

"I told the FBI she left and the general direction she was headed in." Kayla looked in Wade's direction, then back at Jericho and said, "I didn't tell them how I knew, though. They'll probably ask questions later, but right now they're happy to have the information any way they can get it."

"How *did* you know?" Wade asked.

"I activated some intel-gathering tools I already had set up. But I hadn't mentioned them to the feds until now."

Wade's smile was sharp. "Didn't mention them because they weren't quite legitimate?" Jericho wasn't sure how Wade had come to that conclusion so quickly, but Kayla's expression made it clear Wade had guessed right. And Wade was enjoying his victory as he added, "Our little Kay, bending the rules? Say it ain't so!"

"*Bending* the rules is different from smashing them all to shit, Wade!"

"Don't start," Jericho interrupted. "We've got two missing kids, and you both have pieces of the puzzle. Wade, tell her, okay? The same stuff you told me?"

"You want me to talk to the cops, Jay?"

"What the hell else are we doing here? Tell her."

For a long moment Jericho thought Wade was going to refuse. But finally, with a glare in Jericho's direction, Wade started talking.

He gave the abbreviated version, but there was still enough to make Kayla swear. "So has she gone to meet them now?" she demanded. "And me telling the feds—shit, that might have made things worse. They were heading out to find her, but they wouldn't let me or any of my guys go along. They said they had to be discrete. Like a bunch of city assholes in black sedans are going to be less obvious than some locals in pickups or out hiking."

"Your guys *are* getting better at working in the woods," Wade admitted. "Still not really—you know, still not quite *competent*, but better."

"Shut up, Wade." Jericho closed his eyes and tried to think. "Okay, this might not be a terrible thing. If she's gone to the drop, she must have the evidence with her. At least one copy of it. And if the dirty feds know she's being tracked through Sheriff's Department resources, not because she tipped anyone off, they shouldn't overreact about a messed-up drop, right?"

"Maybe," Kayla agreed cautiously.

"So possibly this has bought us some time. It'll be a botched drop, but not one that'll make them panic and hurt the kids." Hopefully he wasn't being overly optimistic.

"What's the long-term plan?" Wade seemed to have refocused on the issue. "For the dirty feds. They know Nikki could make copies of the evidence, so they're not dumb enough to be satisfied with her giving them just one copy. So they're either counting on her not having set up a dead man's switch and they're going to knock her off as soon as they can do it safely, or they've got some better plan to keep her quiet in the long run. Taking the kids . . . it might be an extra level of threat. Like, they're reminding her that they *could* take her kids anytime she doesn't behave."

"That's a gamble, though," Kayla said. "Especially with someone like Nikki. It might make her 'behave,' sure, or it might push her over the edge."

"And they took the kids in a flashy way." Jericho was glad he had other brains working on this problem now. "If they'd just wanted to make a threat, they could have shown up at Eli's house and just waved a gun at them or something. Taking them from the upstanding neighbor's house? That's a move that's guaranteed to get serious police attention."

Kayla paced restlessly. "Good point. Why the hell weren't they more subtle?"

"With Jay in town, it would have been a lot harder to get the kids at the cabin," Wade said. "They might have just gone for an easy target at the neighbors.'"

"Wouldn't have been hard to get me away from the cabin, though. One call from the feds and I would have gone to meet them, and I wouldn't have suspected them if anything bad had happened while I was gone."

"Not unless Nikki gave you the background," Kayla said.

Jericho snorted. "She's shown zero sign of wanting to do that so far."

"They wouldn't know that, though," Kayla pointed out. "For all they know, she could have told you the whole story."

"No. They'd know I didn't know, because I didn't turn them in. And because one of them pumped me for information yesterday outside Wade's bar, and I told him how little I knew. I might even have given him the idea to go after the kids. I said something about Nikki doing whatever was best for them."

"Which agent was that?" Kayla demanded.

"Lachey."

"Damn it, he's one of the nice ones!"

"And he might have just been doing his job. Just asking basic questions. The kids weren't too closely supervised at the house," Jericho said. "Somebody could have grabbed them out of the forest or anywhere else they roam, and Nikki wouldn't have noticed for quite a while. There were easier ways to get them than snatching them from the neighbors."

"So this could have been smoother, and it wasn't," Wade mused. "Maybe it was because of a time crunch—they had to act fast, before Nikki sold the video to someone less vulnerable than she was. Or maybe—" Wade looked at Kayla, then over at Jericho, then back to Kayla before sighing. "Maybe the feds aren't the only crooked cops involved. And maybe the other bent cops are a bit less smooth."

"What others?" Kayla's voice was threatening, but Wade seemed more amused than intimidated.

"What, that's impossible? Your guys are beyond reproach?"

"Even if they weren't, what the hell would it have to do with the current situation?"

"Well, the feds are the ones on the video. At least the video I saw. But Nikki says she's got other videos; maybe some of it shows different cops. Or if the feds are the only ones that get busted, maybe they *know* about other crooked cops. Cops on the take have already broken *one* code of honor, so you've got to assume they'd be snitches if they had reason to be. If these feds go down and they get offered a deal to turn other people in, they'd probably take it. So who would they know about? Who'd want to make sure they had no reason to start talking?"

"You're stretching," Kayla said firmly. "That's just speculation. I mean, what if the feds aren't involved in this at all? What if it's some other small-time gangster trying to scare Nikki into spreading the wealth? Hell, Wade, what if it's *you*?"

"And me coming to Jericho is a clever smoke screen." Wade tented his fingers and tapped the tips together like a clichéd arch-villain. "Busted. Good police work there, Sheriff."

"Nikki froze me out after talking to the FBI," Jericho said, trying to get things back on track. "It's not hard proof, no. But it suggests that they're involved. And like Wade said, evidence like hers wouldn't be that valuable to anyone in town, but it would be devastating to the cops who got recorded. So they're the ones with the strongest motive."

"Them or someone they might rat on." Kayla whirled on Wade. "So? You tell me. Have I got dirty cops in my department?"

He smiled at her. "How'd you track Nikki? Your less-than-legit 'intel gathering.' What's that look like?"

She shook her head. "No. I'm not sharing that information."

Wade raised an eyebrow and sounded almost prim as he replied, "Well, then. I'm sure I couldn't speculate about the members of your department."

That was when Kayla's cell rang. She lifted it to her ear, barked her name into the receiver, and listened for a moment. "Okay, thanks. Keep an eye on it." She frowned at Wade, then said into the phone, "And, Garron? *Just* me. Tell the feds we lost track of her. Tell that to *anyone* who asks. Got it?" She waited for a moment but apparently didn't hear an objection. Then she ended the call and shoved the phone back in her pocket. "She's on the move again. Maybe they pulled out of the first drop because they knew we had her tracked." She whirled to face Wade. "*Garron's* clean, right? There's no way Garron—"

"Garron's too stubborn to be dirty," Wade agreed. "He's a sadistic bastard and a pain in the ass, but he's your best bet."

"And the others?" Jericho didn't want to ask and be refused, but he couldn't just let Wade walk away with information the department needed. "Wade, we need to get this under control. Cops turning a blind eye to some of your stuff or tipping you off on a bust—that's one thing." He looked at Kayla. "It happens in every department. It's not good, but the real problem is that it leads to worse." He turned back to Wade. "There's two kids' lives on the line. *That's* worse. We need to know who's dirty in the department so we know who we can pressure. And we're running out of time, Wade. We don't want to *solve* a child murder, we want to prevent it."

Wade's face was completely expressionless, which had always been a sign that his mind was racing too fast for him to put on an act. Finally, he shrugged. "You want someone who's worked with the bikers, I'd guess. That'd be the connection to the dirty feds, right?"

Jericho nodded cautiously. He was afraid that if he spoke, he'd say the wrong thing and Wade would stop talking.

"So look at Posniewski, Trainor, and maybe Jackson. The first two are definite. I've never been sure about Jackson."

Kayla swallowed hard, but after a moment she jerked her head in a rough nod. "Okay. Posniewski. I can bully him. Haul him into the interrogation room and scare the crap out of him. Except I don't want the feds to see me pushing him. Shit. I'll call him and tell him to meet me somewhere else."

"I'll come with you," Jericho said. "You don't want to be caught alone with him, Kay, not if he's desperate."

She nodded, then turned to Wade. "I'll never crack Trainor. She's as tough as Garron. You think you could reach out to her, see what she spills? You could talk to her as a potential business associate or whatever." Her face was bleak, possibly because she was setting up one of her own deputies, or possibly because she was relying on Wade to do it.

Wade took a moment before saying, "Maybe. Yeah, maybe. What are we hoping to find out, exactly?"

"The most important information is where the kids are," Jericho said firmly. "If we can't get that, we should try to get names for the dirty feds or any locals who might have been involved in the grab, a location for the next drop location for Nikki—anything that might help. Wade and Nikki have both seen the tape—maybe we could have them search through personnel files and do IDs that way. But that'll need federal cooperation and take a while; for now, the kids' location is the priority. I'm going to call my captain in LA and pass all this along, get her to contact whoever she knows in DC. We're running out of time; we can't worry about being subtle anymore."

"We've still got nothing even *close* to evidence," Kayla said. "But, yeah, it'd be good to share what we've got."

Good to share it now because we might not be alive to do it later.

"And before we do all *that* sharing," Wade said, "I think there's something you were going to share with *me*. Sheriff?"

Kayla's lip twitched, and she turned to face Jericho as she spoke. Maybe it was easier to give the information away less directly. "I knew where Nikki was going because I've got a GPS tracker on the truck you rented from Scotty Hawk. He and Wade do business together, and sometimes they take that vehicle, so . . ."

And Wade looked strangely satisfied rather than shocked. Damn it, he looked as if he'd already known about the tracker, or at least suspected, and he'd just wanted to hear Kayla admit to it. In order to humiliate her, or to protect his own pride? He couldn't let himself *give* information to law enforcement, but maybe he could trade for it?

But Jericho didn't have time to sort through Wade's complexities. "So as long as Nikki stays with the truck, we know where she is. And the feds aren't aware of the tracker?"

Kayla shook her head. "It's not exactly approved procedure, and, well, I *thought* the feds were all about procedure."

Jericho tried to fit the new information into his brain. "Could you take Garron with you when you meet with your deputy—Posniewski, was that his name? That would free me up, and I could try to track down Nikki. If she stays with the truck, I'll keep my distance until you can get me some backup, but if she leaves it, I'll follow her and keep you guys in the loop."

"Splitting up seems like a bad idea," Kayla said. "But, damn it, I don't see a way around it. We need to get shit done, and we're running out of time."

"We can stay in touch," Jericho said, holding up his cell phone.

"Just like you stayed in touch *last* time you ditched us?" Wade asked sweetly. He didn't wait for an answer, though, just headed for the edge of the cliff and turned to lower himself over the edge.

Kayla followed him without a word, leaving Jericho to bring up the rear. He wished there was time for more conversation, or at least for a better good-bye, but they had jobs to do. So he swung his legs over the side of the cliff, climbed down until he was almost at the bottom, then let himself fall.

CHAPTER 11

"You'll need to talk to my dad," Kayla told Jericho when they were all at the bottom of the cliff. "He's the one who started setting the trackers, and he still monitors them for me. Best to keep that kind of equipment out of the office, you know?"

"You want me to talk to your dad?" Chasing down dirty feds who'd already killed two people? Okay, Jericho could handle that. But talking to Sheriff Morgan Senior? Damn.

Kayla didn't look too impressed with his reticence. "I'll call him and let him know you're coming. And this is serious, so he'll cooperate, as long as you don't set him off. Don't try to feed him any of that smart-ass crap you were dishing out at the station and you should be okay."

"You were dishing out smart-ass crap at the sheriff's station?" Wade said with a warm smile. "I knew you hadn't changed!"

"He's a cop himself, Wade," Kayla retorted. "He's changed plenty."

"Only on the surface," Wade replied, then tossed his own truck keys to Jericho, saying, "It'll be easier for me to find a loaner than for you to. But I like that truck. Take better care of it than you did the last ones."

It felt wrong to be leaving. Those few minutes of comradeship up by the cave? As rushed as they'd been, as desperate as the situation was, they'd still seemed more real than anything Jericho had experienced since he'd left Mosely so long ago. His squad had covered his ass in the Marines, and the other cops in LA had his back, but that was because of the uniform Jericho had been wearing. He'd been protected because he was a fellow soldier or a fellow cop. Wade and Kayla were on his side because he was *Jericho*. That was an important difference.

Of course, they were also on his side because there were two kids at risk. Jericho set out at a half run through the forest, heading down toward Wade's truck. Wade was at his heels, but they separated when they left the forest, Wade heading back into whatever world he lived in now.

Jericho kept moving, reached the truck, wondered what contraband he'd find if he did a quick search, then got in and started driving. He called his captain in LA as he drove, got her voice mail, and gave as much information as he could. It took him three separate messages, since he kept getting cut off, but there was someone out there who would know where to start looking for answers if things went wrong. But it was best not to think about that.

Kayla's dad still lived in the same house he'd raised Kayla in: a bungalow on the edge of town, its yard backing onto the forest. That proximity to nature had made it easy for Kayla to sneak out and escape through the trees, and Jericho had spent a lot of time in his teenage years hanging out in the woods, waiting for her. But the tree line had always been the unofficial barrier he could not cross. In the forest, he and Kayla had been friends, but she'd never brought him home to the sheriff's house.

Now, it was strange to pull up into the driveway like it was no big thing, especially driving Wade Granger's truck. He knew Kayla had called ahead, but all the same he felt like he should be approaching the house with his hands up.

The front door opened before he reached it, and Sheriff Morgan stood there, waiting with his standard look of disapproval-bordering-on-disgust.

"You're back," he grunted. His hair was grayer and his gut slightly more pronounced, but his back was ramrod straight and his gaze as sharp as ever. "And you're getting Kayla involved in another mess."

"Kayla's the sheriff," Jericho said as mildly as possible. "Dealing with crime is her job."

"She says you're on the force out in Los Angeles." Morgan pronounced the city's name like a disease. "But you need to remember you don't have any damn jurisdiction here, and we do things our own way in Mosely."

"Like the illegal trackers you put on third-party vehicles," Jericho said. "And one of those seems like it might be useful right now. Are you able to give me a mobile device I can use to locate the tracker, or will I need to follow directions you give me remotely?"

Morgan frowned at him. Apparently the proper etiquette would have involved more insults and posturing before any actual business was discussed, but Jericho didn't have time for that crap. Finally, Morgan jerked his head and stepped out of the doorway.

"Get inside," he growled. "We're not going to talk about this in the middle of the damn street."

Jericho followed the man inside, down a hallway lined with all of Kayla's school pictures and a few extras, and then around a corner to the basement stairs.

"You first," Morgan said, pointing toward the stairs.

Yeah, of course. Whoever was on the lower step would be susceptible to an attack from above. It was a matter of principle. So Jericho jogged down the steps, giving in to the man's power games.

When he reached the bottom and gazed out into the large room that should have been a rec room or a workshop or something, he froze.

The place looked like a damn surveillance van: three computers, several stations with headphones and video screens, a big white board with markers at the ready, and a long table in the middle, six chairs on either side and one at each end.

"You running a task force out of your basement, Sheriff Morgan?"

"I do some private security work. Nothing for you to worry about."

But he'd brought Jericho down here to see it all. So a message was being sent, but Jericho wasn't receiving it too well. "Is there a remote receiver I can use, or how are we going to do this?"

Morgan walked past Jericho over to one of the computers and tapped a few keys. He typed faster than most men his age, probably faster than Jericho did. Apparently the retired sheriff wasn't living in the past. Was *that* supposed to be the damn message?

"It's not easy to be a female sheriff in a small town," Morgan said, and there was an accusation in his tone.

"I'm not trying to make it any more difficult," Jericho replied. An overprotective father? Okay, he could work with that.

"Kayla's a smart girl, a strong girl."

Jericho briefly considered making the correction of *girl* to *woman*, but his better sense kept his mouth shut. "She sure seems to be. And following this tracker could really help us out, so—"

"It's my job to help and protect *her*, not you."

Damn it, Jericho was done. "There are two little kids involved in this situation, Mr. Morgan. That's who we *all* need to be helping and protecting, and there's a serious time issue. If you want, I can give you my word that I'll come by after all this is finished and you can yell at me about whatever the hell is up your ass, but right now, I need you to focus on the task at hand. Can you please give me a portable receiver if you have one, or otherwise tell me how you're going to get in touch with me as I'm traveling?"

The old man's eyes narrowed into slits. "You think you can bully me into doing what you want? A punk like you? In my own home?"

"Bully you? Fuck that. But I sincerely hope I can *shame* you into it. You're acting like you're better than me *while* not sharing information that could be used to help two little kids? That's giving you the moral edge, somehow? Bullshit."

"I don't like your mouth, boy. I never have."

"I don't give a shit and never have. Should I call Kayla and tell her we need a plan B, or can you give me the help she promised?"

For a frustrating moment, Jericho was sure the old man was going to call his bluff. But finally he turned away in an elaborate show of disgust, grabbed something off the shelf behind him, and swung back around to thrust it toward Jericho. "Standard GPS screen. I've got it set to receive the signal from the transmitter in question. The green dot will be you, the red dot the target. The dots will turn to arrows if you or the target are in motion. You understand that?"

Jericho nodded and swallowed back his comment about the receiver being incredibly unsophisticated compared to some of the stuff he'd used in the military. He was getting what he wanted, so he should keep his mouth shut. "And you can track from here as well, and relay the information to Kayla?"

"Let me worry about that," Morgan grunted.

Maybe that was all Jericho could hope for, so he turned toward the stairs. "Thanks for this," he said, looking down at the device, his mind already busy with possible routes to follow.

"Crewe," Morgan barked, and Jericho could hear generations of hostility in the man's tone. "Anything happens to my little girl with this—*anything*—and I'm holding you personally responsible."

"She's a grown woman," Jericho said. "But I'll do what I can to keep her safe." That was the best he could promise. For himself, and for anyone else—he'd try.

CHAPTER 12

The GPS signal led Jericho out of town, deep into the woods and halfway up the mountainside. It had been his playground, once, this territory, and despite the urgency of the current situation, it was good to be back, surrounded by trees and nature. Just the day before he'd been uncomfortable driving out to his father's place, but that reticence was already gone. It was as if the oxygen from the vegetation balanced out the thin air from the altitude, and each breath was a reward for his body. And maybe, yeah, maybe, it felt good to be working a case like this, doing something that could make a difference instead of sorting through the tragic remains of homicides back in LA. There, the violence was endemic and his part came after things had already gone inescapably wrong; here, maybe he could actually change things.

So he headed toward the red dot on the receiver and hoped for the best.

He was on a logging road when the dot turned to an arrow and started moving. Coming toward him. *Damn it.* They were on a typical forestry service road, a rough and narrow track into the woods, with no turnoffs, barely anywhere to even turn *around*. Whoever was approaching was going to spot him. He jammed the truck into reverse, bounced backward faster than the ruts on the road justified, and found enough room for a quick three-point turn. The signal from the other truck was only a few hundred yards away, but the road was twisty and heavily forested, so Jericho probably wouldn't be seen.

He thought about blocking the road. If it was just Nikki in the truck, he could demand her cooperation and figure out a better plan. But she might have kidnappers with her, and he couldn't mess up whatever ransom drop they might be working on.

So he raced back to the main road, made an arbitrary decision to turn toward town instead of away, and then slowed down and watched the GPS. The signal reached the intersection, paused, and then turned away from town.

And just like that, Jericho realized where the truck was going. He stopped for a moment to think it through, then sped up without turning around. There used to be a bit of a track just up ahead . . . and there it was. Rougher than it had been, maybe, but still passable. Jericho bounced along on the trail, muttering an apology to Wade's suspension and keeping an eye on the GPS. If he was wrong, he was going to have to back out of there fast. But if he was right . . .

The signal showed Nikki's truck turning off the road and staying exactly where Jericho had predicted. Perfect. He drove farther, until he found a fallen tree across the trail and had to slam on the brakes. The GPS told the story, and it wasn't bad. He was a mile or two from his target, but it was all downhill. Of course if he got down there and then the signal started moving again, he was going to have to hustle to get back up to Wade's truck to follow it.

But he had a feeling this was the final destination. The first location had obviously been intended as the meeting place, but that had been thwarted when the feds found out that Kayla knew where Nikki was. So then the second stop must have been to make sure Nikki wasn't being followed anymore. Maybe she'd met someone there, or picked up instructions; it was frustrating not to know, but there was nothing to be done about that.

Now, though. The copper mine. It had been on its last legs when Jericho had left Mosely, and the toxic water in what was left of the open pit had made national news a few years earlier when a whole flock of migrating birds had died after landing on the lake. Apparently the water was highly corrosive; Jericho tried not to think about how convenient a huge pit of acid would be to someone trying to dispose of child-sized bodies.

He pulled out his cell and dialed as he moved, but there was only one bar of service, and when the call connected he heard only static, and then nothing as the phone gave up trying. Not shocking, considering how far out of town he was, but not great, either.

Texts might not work any better, but he punched in a quick message and sent it to Kayla and Wade. *Tracked signal to copper mine on Westerfield Road. Took the track to the old cabin and will go xcountry from here.* The old cabin where he'd gone to be alone with both Kayla *and* Wade, at different times, but he didn't think he'd mention that in the current context. They'd know what he was talking about, if they ever got the text.

He hit Send and held the phone up as he moved in case the extra couple of feet of altitude might help it find a signal. He'd hope backup was on its way, but if he messed around trying to find a signal or drive back to town, it would be too damn late.

So he skidded down the steep slope, jogging to keep from falling, bouncing off a few trees, wishing he had more firepower than his Glock, just in case things got interesting at the bottom. It would have been comforting to come up with a plan, but he just didn't know enough. He didn't know how many kidnappers there would be, or if the kids were at the mine, or what condition they were in, or whether Nikki was even involved or whether someone else had been driving her truck—

He slowed down and took care as the ground started to level out and light showed through the forest. One last look at the GPS confirmed that the beacon was still dead ahead.

Jericho made sure the ringer on his phone was off, then worked his way forward, using the trees for cover. They were mostly conifers, their wide-spreading branches good for camouflage but not solid enough to stop a shot if he was seen.

His rental truck and a couple of other vehicles were parked in front of the main building, the one he assumed would have been for the mine offices. There were larger buildings he was pretty sure would have held equipment and maybe done some basic ore processing, but the offices seemed like the best place to start looking. He circled around the back, away from the front door where the truck was parked, looking for an alternate entrance.

He found several, but they were all heavy doors with solid locks. He could probably bust through them, but not without making a lot of noise. He scouted around, peeked through windows . . . and saw it. A little plastic dinosaur sitting on the floor of one of the offices.

It wasn't conclusive, wouldn't mean much in court. But it was enough for Jericho. The kids *had* been here, maybe still *were* here. Nikki was here too, or at least the truck she'd been driving was. Yeah, it was enough. Jericho needed to get inside. He tried 911 this time, but got the same lack of signal as before.

He was suddenly grateful for some of the trouble he'd gotten into with Wade when they were younger. There'd never been a door that Wade couldn't lock pick or bust open somehow, but Jericho had tended to be a bit less direct. He looked around and saw the drainpipe running down from the roof, the little overhang over the back door, right next to the pipe . . . that might work.

He didn't give himself time to reconsider, just made sure his phone and weapon were secured and then sprang at the drainpipe. It gave but stayed upright, and he scrambled up it, braced his feet on the overhang, and then climbed the rest of the way to the roof.

And there it was. An access door. Likely still locked, but . . . he eased closer, careful to not make any noise that might be heard below, and smiled as he pulled out his wallet. They'd installed a cheaper lock up here where no one was likely to try to break in. A few slides of his driver's license, a gentle tug, and the door swung open.

He replaced his wallet and pulled out his cell. *I'm going in through a door on the roof,* he texted. Then he traded the phone for his Glock.

The stairs led into a windowless utility room, and Jericho dug his phone back out to use as a flashlight. There was a floor plan by the door, showing both levels of the building and all the emergency exits. He flicked the light switch, but nothing happened. The electricity was off, which wasn't surprising. He hadn't heard a generator, so they were probably depending on flashlights and natural light. Which room would have the best exposure to sunlight? He looked over the plans. The cafeteria, a high-ceilinged space with skylights and a wall of windows. And it was out in front, right beside the parked truck. So that was where people were most likely to be.

Which meant that was where he was going. He didn't let himself think about all the rules he was breaking by going in solo: rules of police work *and* of common sense. He just thought of that dinosaur, lost and alone, and he kept moving.

There was no access to the cafeteria from the second floor, so he found a staircase and worked his way down. He heard the voices soon after he hit the ground floor—he'd been right; they were coming from the cafeteria.

"It's the only copy!" Nikki's voice was high and frightened. "I promise."

Something lower, too quiet to hear, came from what sounded like a man.

Then Nikki said, "I don't have a computer! I don't know *how* to make copies!"

Jericho swore silently. If she convinced whoever she was talking to that she'd given up the only copy of the evidence, then she was the only witness to the crimes; it would be safest to kill her.

Another low rumble before Nikki said, "Just let them go. Okay? This isn't about them. They're good kids. Let them go. It can just be you and me."

Jericho edged closer. The cafeteria had no tables anymore, and no doors, only the doorframes. From where he was standing he could see Nikki, but no one else. With luck, that meant no one else could see him. He made his motions a little bigger, enough to be seen out of the corner of Nikki's eye, and hoped that if she did notice him, her reaction wouldn't give him away.

She glanced in his direction, so quick he wasn't sure she'd seen him, her movement blending into her general level of frenzy. Then she said, "Send the kids outside. Let them go. You and I can deal. If we don't figure something out, you can go catch them again, right? I just don't—I don't want them to see this." So she *had* noticed him and was clearly counting on him to get the kids out of there while she distracted the kidnappers. Distracted them with her own death, from the sounds of her plan. Whatever her other mothering skills were, she certainly seemed strong in the area of protection.

And she was smart too, she reminded him as she kept talking. "There's three of you," she said. "Plus that guy in the back room with the kids, behind you. You can't seriously think you wouldn't be able to handle me without having my children here? And if you had to find them, you could, easy."

Valuable information. Jericho needed to pass it along. *Four perps on site*, he texted. *One adult, two child vics. Scene not secure. Backup requested.* He had no idea if Kayla or Wade were getting these messages, but at least he was doing what he could.

He was close enough now to hear the man's response. "The kids stay here," he said. "You *all* stay here."

That was when Nikki pulled the device out of her pocket, flipped the lid, and depressed the button with her thumb. "Detonator," she said, the fear gone from her voice, replaced with fierce determination. "That truck out there? Under the tarp in the back? Sixty pounds of C-4. Military grade. You know Eli was running that stuff across the border. And now it's ready to smash through those windows and take us all out if my kids don't walk away from here, *now*."

Jesus. She hadn't bothered with a *virtual* dead man's switch because she'd had the real thing in her pocket the entire time.

"You're bluffing," the man said. "You'd be killing your own kids."

"Better me than you. And I'm hoping with the wall between us, and them being closer to the ground . . . I'm hoping it'll protect them. But even if it doesn't, *better me than you*." She sounded deadly serious as she ordered, "You let them go *now*."

"You're a crazy bitch, you know that?" The male voice was growing louder, approaching Nikki. Shit. Should he lean out to get a better view of the man or pull farther back into the little alcove he'd found to shelter from any blast that might be coming? What would the effect of sixty pounds of C-4 be? He wasn't an explosives expert and didn't know much about the building structure, but sixty pounds of C-4? It would turn the truck into shrapnel, the windows into shrapnel, and could definitely collapse the side of the building if it were packed in tight enough.

"Let my kids go," Nikki demanded.

Then there was the *crack* of a handgun firing. Nikki staggered, fought to stay on her feet, and then a man was on her, grabbing her hand and wrestling the detonator away. *Damn it.*

Jericho strode forward, Glock ready. "Freeze," he ordered. "Police."

The man had the detonator in one hand, and now he raised the other, pointing a gun toward Jericho. Damn it, now *he* had the dead man's switch. If Jericho shot him—

"Shoot!" Nikki screamed, and Jericho did—two hits, right in the chest. An instant bloom of red—no vest. But as he fell, the detonator dropped from his hand. It was falling, but Nikki wasn't moving. She wasn't even bracing herself.

Jericho strode forward, making it to the doorway while the other two men were running for cover. "Police," Jericho bellowed. He wasn't sure about jurisdiction, but the other guys clearly weren't too worried about it. "Drop your weapons."

One of them seemed to have figured out that there wasn't going to be an explosion. He turned, raised his gun—and Jericho fired two bullets, one into the man's shoulder, the other his chest. Two down.

But two to go, assuming Nikki's count had been accurate. The third man from the cafeteria was gone, somewhere, and there was still the man who was with the kids.

Jericho crouched beside Nikki, keeping most of his attention on the far end of the room while sneaking quick looks at the oozing red hole in her leg. "You were bluffing about the C-4?"

"Lot of good it did me."

He slipped his belt out through the loops of his jeans. "This is going to hurt," he warned.

"Go get my kids," she gasped.

"I will. Let me just . . ." He lifted her thigh as gently as he could to slide the belt underneath her. There weren't enough holes to secure the tourniquet, so he cinched it tight and then handed her the end. "Keep pulling on that. Keep it snug." And that was all he could do for her, at least for the time being. "Do you know where they're keeping Elijah and Nicolette?"

She shook her head. "They're here. I saw them before I handed over the thumb drive. But I don't know where they went."

"That direction?" Jericho asked, nodding his head toward the doors the man had run through.

Nikki managed a nod.

"Okay. Sit tight. I'll see what I can do."

He was probably going to get himself killed. He'd lost the element of surprise, didn't know the layout of the building, and there were children to be used as hostages or human shields. But he went anyway, checking his Glock and then moving fast and careful toward the exit the man had taken.

There was no sign of him in the first hallway. A stairwell off to the right, a long corridor to the left; the guys would want to avoid getting trapped on the second floor if they could, so Jericho turned left. It wasn't much more than a guess, but when he heard a muffled crash from somewhere down by the end of the hall, he liked his choice.

He moved as quickly as he could without being careless. It would have been better to have a team, someone to watch his back and cover him when he took chances, but he couldn't afford to let the kidnappers get away, not until Elijah and Nicolette were safe. With a situation gone this far sideways, the kidnappers' instinct would be to kill the kids and get the hell out of Dodge. Jericho wasn't going to let that happen.

So he jogged forward, handgun ready. Halfway down the hall there was a new corridor running off to the left. Jericho pressed his back against the wall opposite the opening and edged sideways along the wall, trying to get a better view. Then he caught a voice, clearly a child's, raised in wordless protest. It was coming from right around the corner.

"Shut the fuck up," a man ordered, and Jericho leapt into the intersection, gun raised. Goddamn it. Lachey, both hands busy with a struggling child. The kid was moving too fast for Jericho to be sure which one it was.

"Police," Jericho yelled. "Lachey, step away from the kid and keep your hands where I can see them."

Of course it didn't work. The guy turned so he was behind the kid, got a better grip, and lifted the small, twisting body up with an arm around the throat. "We're walking out of here," he growled.

"Fine. I've got an injured woman to take care of; I'm interested in the kids, not you. You leave them behind and you can go anywhere you want."

"With you chasing after me, telling everyone I'm involved."

"Jesus, Lachey, I already did. I gave your name to my captain in LA. The sheriff knows. There are witnesses who've seen the videos, and they'll be able to pick you out of a photo lineup. This is over. You're busted. There's no reason to hurt children."

That was when Jericho caught a blur in the corner of his eye. Someone from farther down the original hallway. And then action from even farther down the hall—damn it, was there a fifth perp?

Jericho was starting to shift when something hit his shoulder. Like a hard punch, but sharper, deeper.

There was no pain for a moment, just impact and shock before he realized what had happened. Lachey had shot him. The fucker was taking the nuclear option, going out fighting. Jericho was down. He'd failed. Then the pain hit and brought rage with it.

These bastards. These—Jericho was halfway to the floor when he saw the kidnapper down the hall stumble forward, his chest blossoming red. No time to ask questions; Jericho found his willpower, his damn Crewe stubbornness, and he turned and raised his gun.

"Drop the kid," he roared at Lachey, his voice stronger than his knees. He recognized Nicolette, now, and saw his own anger echoed on her face. So he wasn't totally shocked when one of her skinny legs lifted and then pistoned backward, her foot slamming Lachey right in the crotch.

The agent dropped her, pointed his gun at her, and Jericho took the shot. Clean in the chest, but Jericho fired again just to make sure.

He glanced back down the hallway toward the other kidnapper. He was down, and Wade Granger was easing forward, shotgun at the ready. "You okay?" Wade asked.

"I'm standing," Jericho managed. But he couldn't lift his left arm, and he was losing a fair bit of blood. "We *should* be clear now, but don't count on it."

"I never do." Wade came closer, squinted at Jericho, then turned to Nicolette. "Where's your brother?"

"Fuck you!" the little girl snarled. She glared at Jericho. "He said he was police!"

Jesus. Jericho didn't want to think what this kid's future was going to be like, with that level of suspicion and hatred already worked into her. Then again, it was probably that same anger that had made her tough enough to fight back. And her eyes had darted toward a room across the hall as soon as Wade had asked the question, anyway.

Maybe in a year or two she'd have that reflex under control, but for now it was useful.

Jericho stumbled toward the door and pushed it. It was heavy, hard to open . . . and then he heard a grunt on the far side. Elijah was holding the door shut. Damn it, these kids were fighters. Jericho could have gotten the door open just by falling on it, but maybe the kid needed a chance to make his own decision on this one. "Hey, buddy. It's Jericho. Your brother. Remember, your mom introduced us? She's here, but she's hurt. I want to take you guys to her, and then get her to the doctor. Can you help me with that?"

Jericho's shoulder was a weird mix of pain and numbness, and he wasn't going to wait very long for Elijah to think things over; luckily, he didn't need to. The door shifted a little and a pair of wide eyes appeared at about Jericho's knee level. The kid had been sitting with his back against the door. "Where's Mom?"

Jericho nodded, the motion continuing inside long after his head stilled. "She's back down the hall. Let's go find her."

Elijah stood, and Jericho forced himself to start walking. He stumbled, had trouble catching himself, and then Wade was there, strong and warm, tucking himself under Jericho's uninjured shoulder and straightening them both up. "Cavalry should be here soon," Wade said. "Hang in there."

Jericho tried to nod. He was starting to feel a bit dizzy. A bit removed from it all. He tried to walk, managed a rough lurch, and then felt himself fading. He wasn't going to be able to hold on.

But Wade was there. Jericho was leaving again, far too soon, but this time, at least, Wade was with him. "I can't . . ." he started, but wasn't sure the words came out of his mouth before he was sliding, falling. But it was okay, because Wade's strong arms were wrapped around him, and he could still feel them even after all the rest of the world had faded away.

CHAPTER 13

"The evidence is gone." Kayla's voice was laced with frustration, an organic anger that cut through the cold sterility of the hospital room. "We searched the whole place, and every dead body that came out of it. If there was a thumb drive, there isn't anymore."

Jericho squinted and tried to concentrate. He was alive, shockingly enough, so he needed to make himself useful. The hospital was weaning him off the strongest painkillers, but he was still a little fuzzy in the brain. "She said 'thumb drive,' but whatever—if it was on a CD or something—"

"No," Kayla said. "There's nothing. Nothing digital."

"What's Nikki say?"

Kayla's frown turned to a bitter smile. "She has no idea what we're talking about. Video evidence of police corruption? Why would an innocent citizen like her have such a thing?"

Jericho's head was managing to throb despite the pharmaceuticals. "So why does she say she was out there? What was she going to trade for the kids?"

"She has no idea what the kidnappers wanted. She went there because they told her to. That's all. She had no plan."

Great. No evidence, and the only witness wasn't cooperating. The other witnesses were dead, courtesy of him and Wade. "Wade saw one of the clips."

Kayla's expression was hard to read now. "Apparently not," she said carefully. "Apparently he's never heard of it, either. I confronted him about it; he said he didn't know what I was talking about—I wish I'd recorded the goddamn conversation on the cliff. Except then I'd have recorded . . ."

Jericho stared at her. Was Wade just being a pain in the ass? That was entirely possible. But if he wasn't, what was he up to? "We don't know which feds were on the tape. We don't know if the dead ones are the only ones involved. Have you found any other evidence?"

"The feds are handling it themselves. And they're helping me with the deputies. I got a confession out of Posniewski, and they've got him in protective custody now, trying to get more from him."

"So it was the local guys who started all this? It was them who got sloppy, and the feds took over to try to tidy up?"

"That's our working theory. We're still conducting interrogations, trying to get deals brokered, hunting for more evidence . . . you know the drill."

"I've only been in here for two and a half days. You've been busy." And she did look tired, he realized. But still strong and determined. That was Kayla.

She just shrugged. "It's stuff that needs to be done. But it'd be a hell of a lot easier if I could find that damn video."

Jericho tried to think it through. "In the cafeteria, Nikki said she'd given it to the first perp. The first one I shot. She said that— Yeah, she said it before she knew I was there, so she wasn't putting on a show for me. And he didn't argue."

"Okay. So she gave it to him. He either gave it to someone else, or he still had it when you shot him."

"Yeah. Maybe he handed it off? Nikki said there were four perps total. She said that *after* she knew I was there, but she was trying to help me save her kids' lives. I don't think she'd have lied about it, and she'd have had no reason to help a fifth kidnapper get away."

"So we assume she was telling the truth. So the guy in the cafeteria either kept it, or he gave it to someone else who *also* died at the scene."

"So one way or another, it shouldn't have left the building. You're *sure* it's not hidden somewhere?"

"The search has been thorough. And conducted by crime-scene guys, not active-duty cops—no reason to believe any of them are crooked, or connected with anything dirty."

"So someone *else* took it out of the building."

"And we know that Wade Granger is lying about its existence," Kayla said quietly. She watched as Jericho heard the words, and he tried his best not to give her a reaction. "I know he was your friend in the past. I know he saved your life a few days ago. I get that. But, Jay— he's a criminal. And, look, I'm sorry, but this mess has made the feds a bit less closed off about their other investigations, and I've seen their notes on your father's murder. Nikki's statement shows that your dad was going to a meeting with *Wade* when he got pushed off that cliff. They have testimony that Wade and Eli had been disagreeing about something in the last few weeks. Sounds like Wade thought Eli ripped him off. That's definitely worth killing for, in Wade's world."

Jericho let the words sink in. He'd never asked Wade directly about his father's death. The trouble with Nikki, yes, and Wade had denied involvement. But they hadn't said much about Eli. Jericho had been afraid to ask. And now, hearing it . . .

Shit. Eli had been a criminal, a total bastard, but he'd been Jericho's father. Elijah and Nicolette's father. He'd been a human being, and someone had killed him. Wade.

Jericho couldn't think about it right then. He needed some damn peace, needed to get off the drugs so his mind was clear. In the meantime, he'd try to focus on the more immediate concerns.

"Wade lifted the evidence," he said slowly. "I can't remember too much after getting shot. I know we went back to the cafeteria . . ."

"That's where we found you," Kayla confirmed. "You and Nikki were both unconscious. Wade was waiting patiently. He tried to walk out once we arrived, but we stopped him and brought him in for questioning. He was searched, but only for weapons, not for something he could have shoved in his damn wallet."

"Why would he want it?"

"I don't know, Jay. But I was wondering if you might be interested in helping me find out."

He frowned at her. "I think my work here is done. The kids are safe. I should check with Nikki, I guess—if she's feeling secure, that'll mean everyone on the recording is dead or arrested. Other than that? I got shot. I was planning to go back to LA as soon as the doctors spring me and you guys give me the okay to leave town."

"And what's waiting for you in LA?" She'd been standing by the window, but now she came over to his hospital bed. "Because I could really use you here, Jay. I've got a corrupt department—Posniewski's been dirty since my dad's time, from the sound of things, and I'm not sure he's the only one. Wade's saying he got nothing out of Trainor, but then how the hell did he beat me out to the old mine, when I came as soon as I got your texts? Wade and Trainor are denying any sort of corruption on their parts, and of course nobody else is talking. I need someone I can trust."

"You've got Garron."

"Garron's solid. But he's old and slow and killing time until retirement. He's not going to be enough. We haven't found anything on Jackson, but he's so damn political he's useless in any case—every decision he makes is based on whether it'll earn him votes so he can take my job, not on doing the right thing."

"Jesus, Kay." Jericho was back to wishing for more painkillers. "What about the feds? Or the state. They'll have anticorruption departments, won't they?"

"They'll help me tear things apart, I expect. But what I need is someone to help me put things back together." She waited, probably for the next objection, then sighed. "And it's not just me. Nikki's in the hospital for another week at least. The kids are in temporary foster care, but it's not a great placement. They'll be okay spending the nights there, but it'd be best if there was someone else—someone *family*—keeping an eye on them. They've been through a lot, and neither one of them is quick to trust."

"You think they trust *me*?"

"I think they will if Nikki tells them to. And I think she'll tell them to if the other option is them having nobody looking out for them."

"You've got this all thought out, huh?"

Kayla smiled blandly. "Once Nikki's out of the hospital, she's not going to be on her feet right away. She'll need help, and she's too proud and stubborn to take it from most people. But I think you being family will give her an excuse to take it from you." She must have seen Jericho's expression, because she quickly held up her hands. "I'm not saying you have to move in with them or anything. Just . . . be around. Check in and make sure they've got groceries. Try to keep Nikki under control."

"Like that's possible."

"It'll be a challenge," Kayla agreed. "But the other option? Jay, those kids . . . they're not going to make it. They're not like you. I mean, I still don't quite understand how *you* got out of Mosely, out of that life, but you've got to know it was a long shot. And these two, without help? They won't even make it as far as Wade has. He's a criminal, but he's more-or-less sane, most of the time; he's got some self-control, some ability to take care of himself. But without help, Nikki's kids are going to end up just like she was before Eli scraped her out of the gutter and tried to fix her up. I think you know how I feel about your dad, so you'll know how bad off Nikki was when I say that moving in with Eli was a huge step up for her."

Jay looked out the window. He could feel the hands grabbing at him, trying to pull him back into Mosely. He just couldn't figure out if they were going to claw him to death or wrap him in a warm hug. "I don't know," he said. "I could talk to my captain, see if I could take a leave or something for a few months. Just to get things settled down—with your department and with the kids."

Kayla nodded. "Excellent. Thanks, Jay." She turned away from the bed briefly, then turned back. "Your captain mentioned the possibility of lending you to us for six months, when I spoke to her. She said you'd probably be on administrative leave most of that time if you went back, so you might as well be out here doing something useful. I guess they take it pretty seriously out there when one of their officers kills three federal agents? And, coincidentally, the county commissioners here agreed to add an under-sheriff's position for six months. So maybe six months would work for you? At least to start?"

"Jesus, Kayla! When'd you get so pushy? I haven't agreed to this—I just said I'd *talk* about it."

He was half-joking, just trying to buy himself time to catch up to it all, but the look she threw at him made it clear she wasn't amused. "I've got four dead feds and a corrupt sheriff's department. I need someone I can trust to have my back. So if I have to be a little *pushy*? To save my life? I'm gonna push, Jay. Sorry if you don't like it."

And there it was. Kayla was tough, but she was only human, and she was stretched beyond her limits. If he walked away and anything happened to her, would he be able to live with that? "You realize I haven't done any actual police work since I got here. I got lied to by Nikki, tracked the signal you gave me, shot a few guys, got shot myself—"

"You got the job done. That's what I need."

"Those kids, Kay—they're animals. And they hate me. They're dangerous, hostile animals."

"Four dead feds and a corrupt sheriff's department and you're scared of the *children*?"

"Have you met them?"

"Briefly. When I drove them from the crime scene to the foster family." She raised her hand and showed him the bandage. "The boy bites."

"*Elijah* bit you? I thought he was the nice one."

"I'm sure they're both lovely." Kayla grinned. "Deep down." Then she pulled out a stack of papers with a folded leather case on top. It looked a lot like the wallet that held Jericho's LAPD detective shield.

"Would you even be allowed to hire me? I'd be on leave in LA, but out here I can get hired for a whole new job? A job with management responsibility."

"We don't have the same size hiring pool up here. Your military record and your years of service in LA count for a lot. And, strangely enough, the DEA is vouching for you."

"The DEA?" Jericho tried to find a way for that to make sense. "Hockley and Montgomery?"

"They said they've been digging into your background ever since you arrived, and they haven't found a damn thing to worry about. Since their investigative skills are obviously beyond reproach, they're saying you must be clean."

Jesus. Were they trying to do him a favor, or just enjoying the thought of Jericho stuck in Mosely? Stuck in—wait a minute— "This would be a pay cut. I get that, and okay, I can work around it. But . . . would I be in *uniform*?"

Another smile. "I do love a man in beige."

She left then, and Jericho collapsed back into his pillow.

He'd worked so hard: To get out of Mosely, to make a career for himself, a *place* for himself. He'd left everything in Montana behind in order to survive. And now Kayla wanted him to come back.

To help her solve a problem that she hadn't known she had before he showed up, and that she could probably go back to ignoring if she really wanted to. To be with two kids he barely knew and really didn't want to know better. It was crazy. She was out of her mind for even suggesting it. He was crazy for considering it.

He sat up and swung his legs out of bed, then stood and made sure his ass was more-or-less covered. It didn't hurt to walk, not as long as he remembered not to move his arm. They'd said they'd give him a sling when they released him. Maybe it was time they got going with that. He made his way toward the nurses' station.

He was standing there, waiting, when he saw the kids coming toward him. He barely recognized them. They were wearing clean clothes and their blond hair was washed and combed; it seemed like Elijah's had been cut, and Nicolette's was pulled back in a tight braid. They were being escorted by a tired-looking woman wearing a long-sleeved dress, like she might be a member of one of those old-school religious groups. As the kids walked past, both of them stared at him, their eyes wary and almost hostile.

Then Elijah gave him a nod. Barely noticeable, even to Jericho; the woman they were with certainly didn't pay any attention. It was just the tiniest acknowledgment, the suggestion of an acquaintanceship. That was all. Jericho nodded back.

Nicolette didn't give him even that much. But after they'd passed, she reached her hand back behind her head, middle finger extended in a clear and unmistakable greeting of her own. Then she reached a little further down, found the elastic binding her hair, and jerked it loose, letting it fall to the ground behind her as she walked on.

Elijah's quiet dignity, Nicolette's equally quiet rebellion; they both spoke to Jericho at a deeper level than he wanted to contemplate right then. Instead, he turned to the nurse who'd finally arrived to help him. "You said I could get out of here this afternoon. Is there anything we can do to speed that up?"

CHAPTER 14

Jericho gave himself one night in the motel before heading for the airport. He needed a little rest. Given the shortage of healthy mourners, Nikki had opted against a funeral for Eli, and Jericho didn't feel any need to visit the old man's grave. So that was over with. He wasn't sure if the simplicity of the interment made him feel relief or if it was just another depressing reminder of Eli's pathetic life.

Jericho'd managed to get the rental truck back from the mine site, so at least he had wheels. That was one positive. And he'd arranged with Scotty to leave it at the airport, so that was another bright spot. Things were coming together.

Then he turned into the parking lot of Wade's bar, and the tiny glimmer of confidence left him. The place didn't even sell food, so he couldn't pretend he was going there for breakfast. No, this was something else, and he had no idea how it was going to go.

Still, he pulled the heavy door open and made his way inside the too-familiar building. There were already three men drinking at one of the tables, and the same huge bartender was standing in front of the row of liquor bottles.

This time he was marginally friendlier. Or at least more active. When he saw Jericho, he picked up an old-fashioned phone with a curly cord, hit a button, and then said into the mouthpiece, "Your cop friend is here."

Jericho smiled. "You're not even going to *try* to sell me a drink? Come on, not even a breakfast beer?"

"Wade's waiting for you in the office," the bartender said.

So Jericho made himself move. It was stupid to be reluctant. This was what he'd come for, after all. He needed to ignore the memories that sprang at him from every corner of the dim bar, forget the times he and Wade had spent in the back room, playing pool and drinking and sneaking looks and later gropes whenever they thought they could get away with it. That was all in the past, and Jericho needed to let it go.

So he knocked efficiently on the office door, pushed it open, and then tried to ignore the way his whole body sang when he saw Wade. Lust was not a good reason for making life decisions, and neither was nostalgia.

"Good to see you mobile," Wade said with a slow smile. He was sitting behind the desk, his feet propped up on its battered wood, and he didn't stand now. His whole body was balanced, though, ready to move. He wasn't wary, but he was interested. Yeah, Jericho knew Wade too well. The man wanted to see what came next in their little game.

"I'm only walking thanks to you." There was no point in denying it; Wade had saved his life.

"Can't help noticing you didn't repay me by *returning my truck*."

"I was kind of laid up. Kayla said you went and got it." Jericho dug the keys out of his pocket. "Sorry I didn't return it myself, but at least I didn't wreck it."

"And you got Scotty's truck back too," Wade said, as if pleased that Jericho was mending his irresponsible ways. Then he raised an eyebrow. "And I heard you're using it to take yourself to the airport."

Of course he'd heard. "Yeah," Jericho said noncommittally.

"And you just came by to say good-bye?"

"Mostly. But also—Kay's in a bind, Wade. She needs the video from that thumb drive. She needs to know which feds are dirty. Beyond the dead ones, obviously." In the best-case scenario one of them was still alive, so she could lean on him to find out who was dirty in *her* department. "And I thought maybe you could help her with that."

"Me?" Wade's innocent face had always somehow conveyed an added message of *fuck you*. It felt wrong for Jericho to be the recipient of that message.

"You said it wouldn't be all that valuable to you," Jericho pressed. "And it would mean a lot to her."

"And she sent you to ask for it?"

"Not exactly."

"But you're supposed to be my weak spot? I'm supposed to do anything you want, if you just ask nicely enough?"

"I think she'd say it was more the other way around," he said, and immediately wished he hadn't spoken.

But there was no turning back time. Wade rose to his feet in one graceful movement, and he was around the desk almost instantly without seeming to rush. "I'm *your* weak spot? That's what she thinks?"

"I don't know. Maybe."

Wade nodded slowly. "Is that true, Jay? Will you do anything I want, if I just ask nicely enough?"

Jericho made himself swallow. "No." And then, "Not *anything*."

Wade moved closer. Close enough that if either of them had leaned in, just a little, they would have been touching. Jericho fought his rebellious body and made himself stay upright. He wasn't strong enough to step away entirely.

"I don't care about the video," Wade said quietly, and it took a moment for Jericho's addled brain to even remember what he was talking about.

"Okay," Jericho managed. "So, you'll give it back to Kay?"

Wade was still close, and his breath was warm on Jericho's neck as he said, "I care about other things."

Jericho stood, frozen, waiting.

And Wade took half a step back. "Like the extensive business contacts Eli added to that drive. The routes through the forest, the drop spots, the vendors and suppliers on both sides of the border." Wade smiled. "Someone else started the list, but some of them are Eli's, for sure. It's a damn treasure trove. There's enough information, enough potential, to keep a dozen men busy. Eli was too old to do the legwork, but that doesn't mean he didn't know people. And now there are opportunities, Jay. Chances for an enterprising man—or men—to make a lot of money."

Jericho stared at Wade and tried to refocus. He needed to get his blood flowing to his brain again, instead of the more interesting places it had been going. "That's—that's not something you need to tell me about. I only want the video."

"And I want a partner." Wade looked impatient now. "What the hell are you doing, being a *cop*? You're Jericho *Crewe*, for fuck's sake! And what are you doing in LA? You know you're a mountain boy. You were always the one dragging *me* out on hikes and camping and whatever woodsy bullshit you came up with. You could do that for a living, man! Hike up to the border and drop shit off, pick shit up, hike back down—shazam, you've made thousands of dollars, all because you had the sense to ignore an imaginary line a bunch of politicians decided to draw through *your* damn forest."

Wade was speaking with the zeal of a true believer, but there was no way to tell if the idealism ran any deeper than the surface. "And not exclusively grunt work, Jay. I mean it, I need a partner. Someone who'll yell at me when I need it. Someone with a brain and guts. Someone I can *trust*."

That last part that stung. Because Wade should be able to trust Jericho. That was the way it always should be. "I already have a job," Jericho made himself say.

"In LA? Fuck it, Jay. Get your ass back here where you belong." Wade stepped close again. "You've been away too damn long," he said quietly.

This time, Jericho found the strength to step away. "Not in LA." He pulled out the little leather pouch and flipped it open, showing the badge. "Here. For Kay. I'm going to LA to tidy things up, and then I'm coming here to be the under-sheriff for the Mosely County Sheriff's Department."

Wade stared. For a moment, Jericho was pretty sure Wade was going to take a swing at him, and with Jericho's arm out of action, it wouldn't be anything close to a fair fight. Instead, Wade stepped back, and he laughed. It was loud, but not raucous. It was *true*. It was *real*. It was *Wade*, and Jericho should have been able to hear it without wanting to cry.

"Jesus, Jay," Wade finally said. He shook his head with a sort of amused admiration. "Jesus. You really— You just can't do things the easy way, can you?"

"Not usually," Jericho admitted, although he wasn't quite sure what Wade meant in this particular case. "But Kay needs help. And Nikki and the kids, they need some stability. They're *not* going to get that from someone running around in the woods smuggling drugs and weapons across the damn border." And the next part was tricky, but important. "This isn't about you, Wade. I mean, I don't *want* it to be. You said your trouble was mostly with the feds, and I'm hoping we can maintain that. If Kay pushes me to— Well, if she wants me to ask you to cooperate, I'll probably ask you to cooperate. But I don't plan to, I don't know, to—"

"You don't plan to betray me?" Wade's face still showed the traces of his laughter, but his voice was gentle. "That's nice to hear. I don't want to be your enemy, Jay. I don't want us to be on different sides of this."

Yeah, that sounded nice in theory. "We're on different sides. I'm sworn to uphold the law, and you seem bound and determined to break it at every opportunity. So we're on different sides." Jericho looked at the man in front of him. "But, no, I don't want to be your enemy."

Wade's smile was a little sad now. "I guess that's a start. Under-sheriff Crewe." He shook his head, then raised an eyebrow. "Hey. Does that mean you're going to wear the uniform?"

"Apparently."

Wade's eyes danced. "Damn. *That's* something to look forward to."

And that was it. Jericho backed out, drove to the airport, and left the truck where he and Scotty had agreed. He felt a bit empty, as if he was leaving something important behind, but he reminded himself that he was only going to be gone for a few days, and that made things better, and then he started worrying about what the hell *that* meant, that he was feeling better about his imminent return to chaos and confusion.

He was about to turn off his phone for the flight when he got the text from Kayla.

Video just emailed to us from an anonymous account. Call me as soon as you can. We've got work to do.

Jericho reread the message a couple of times, then stuffed the phone in his pocket and leaned back in his seat. There was a warmth in his chest, an ease spreading out through his entire body.

Wade had sent the video. Wade was— What the hell was he? Helping out? Not because he believed in the cause, that was certain.

Maybe it was because Jericho *was* his weak spot. Which made it a hell of a lot easier for Jericho to accept that Wade was his.

It was bewildering, but everything about Wade always had been. As a kid, Jericho had survived Wade by abandoning all hope of control and just giving in to the moment. As a man, Jericho couldn't do that. He had responsibilities, and his own goals and values.

But Wade had sent Kayla the video, and he'd done it because Jericho had asked him to. As gestures went, it was a strange one.

It wasn't much.

It didn't mean anything, really.

But it was enough to keep a smile on Jericho's face for the entire plane ride back to LA.

Explore more of the *Common Law* series at:
riptidepublishing.com/titles/universe/common-law

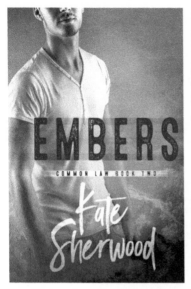

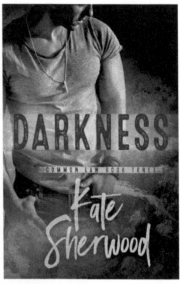

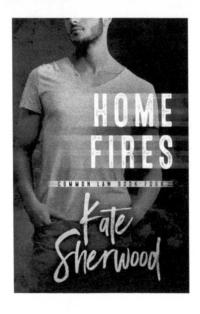

Dear Reader,

Thank you for reading Kate Sherwood's *Long Shadows*!

We know your time is precious and you have many, many entertainment options, so it means a lot that you've chosen to spend your time reading. We really hope you enjoyed it.

We'd be honored if you'd consider posting a review—good or bad—on sites like **Amazon, Barnes & Noble, Kobo, Goodreads, Twitter, Facebook, Tumblr,** and your blog or website. We'd also be honored if you told your friends and family about this book. Word of mouth is a book's lifeblood!

For more information on upcoming releases, author interviews, blog tours, contests, giveaways, and more, please sign up for our weekly, spam-free newsletter and visit us around the web:

Newsletter: tinyurl.com/RiptideSignup
Twitter: twitter.com/RiptideBooks
Facebook: facebook.com/RiptidePublishing
Goodreads: tinyurl.com/RiptideOnGoodreads
Tumblr: riptidepublishing.tumblr.com

Thank you so much for Reading the Rainbow!

RiptidePublishing.com

ALSO BY

KATE SHERWOOD

(all m/m – for m/f see Cate Cameron at catecameronauthor.com)

ABOUT THE
AUTHOR

Kate Sherwood started writing about the same time she got back on a horse after almost twenty years away from riding. She'd like to think she was too young for it to be a midlife crisis, but apparently she was ready for some changes!

Kate grew up near Toronto, Ontario, and went to school in Montreal, then Vancouver. But for the last decade or so she's been a country girl. Sure, she misses some of the conveniences of the city, but living close to nature makes up for those lacks. She's living in Ontario's "cottage country"—other people save up their time and come to spend their vacations in her neighborhood, but she gets to live there all year round!

Since her first book was published in 2010, she's kept herself busy with novels, novellas, and short stories in almost all the subgenres of m/m romance. Contemporary, suspense, sci-fi, or fantasy— the settings are just the backdrop for her characters to answer the important questions: How much can they share, and what do they need to keep? Can they bring themselves to trust someone, after being disappointed so many times? Are they brave enough to take a chance on love?

Kate's books balance drama with humor, angst with optimism. They feature strong, damaged men who fight themselves harder than they fight anyone else. And, wherever possible, there are animals: horses, dogs, cats ferrets, squirrels . . . sometimes it's easier to bond with a nonhuman, and most of Kate's men need all the help they can get.

With her writing, Kate is still learning, still stretching herself, and still enjoying what she does. She's looking forward to sharing a lot more stories in the future. (And check out her imaginary friend, Cate Cameron, who writes m/f romance and YA.)

Enjoy more stories like
Long Shadows
at RiptidePublishing.com!

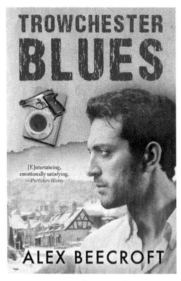

Trowchester Blues
ISBN: 978-1-62649-199-1

The Two Gentlemen of Altona
ISBN: 978-1-62649-219-6

Earn Bonus Bucks!

Earn 1 Bonus Buck for each dollar you spend. Find out how at
RiptidePublishing.com/news/bonus-bucks.

Win Free Ebooks for a Year!

Pre-order coming soon titles directly through our site and you'll
receive one entry into a drawing for a chance to win free books for
a year! Get the details at RiptidePublishing.com/contests.

CPSIA information can be obtained
at www.ICGtesting.com
Printed in the USA
LVHW04s1433151018
593653LV00004B/824/P